Choosing Jesus
The Real Deal on the Spiritual Menu

Leader's Guide

Tim Gossett

Abingdon Press

Choosing Jesus
The Real Deal on the Spiritual Menu

LEADER'S GUIDE

Copyright © 2003 by Abingdon Press.

All rights reserved.

With the exception of those items so noted, no part of this work may be reproduced or transmitted in any form or by any means, electronic or mechanical, including photocopying and recording, or by any information storage or retrieval system, except as may be expressly permitted by the 1976 Copyright Act or in writing from the publisher. Requests for permission should be addressed to Abingdon Press, 201 Eighth Avenue, South, P.O. Box 801, Nashville, TN 37202-0801.

This book is printed on acid-free, recycled paper.

Unless otherwise noted, Scripture quotations are from the *New Revised Standard Version of the Bible,* copyright © 1989, Division of Christian Education of the National Council of the Churches of Christ in the United States of America. Used by permission. All rights reserved.

Scriptures noted *The Message* are taken from THE MESSAGE: Copyright © Eugene H. Peterson, 1993, 1994, 1995. Used by permission of NavPress Publishing Group.

03 04 05 06 07 08 09 10 11 12—10 9 8 7 6 5 4 3 2 1

MANUFACTURED IN THE UNITED STATES OF AMERICA

Development Team
Jola Bortner
Rusty Cartee
Harriette Cross
Tim Gossett
Sharon Meads
Beth Miller
David Stewart

Editorial Team
Crystal A. Zinkiewicz, Senior Editor
Pam Shepherd, Production Editor

Design Team
Keely J. Moore, Design Manager

Administrative Staff
Neil M. Alexander, Publisher
Harriet Jane Olson, Vice President/Editor of Church School Resources
Bob Shell, Director of Youth Resources

Contents

Session 1: Back to the Basics 7

Session 2: Beyond Wings and Halos—
A Look at Angels in the Bible 13

Session 3: Misled and Misleading: Cults 19

Session 4: Children of the One God: Judaism and Islam . .25

Session 5: Faith in a Hurting World: Buddhism 31

Session 6: Equal in the Sight of God: Hinduism 37

Session 7: The Christ Way: Love, Kindness, and Mercy . .43

Reproducible Pages 49

A Retreat: All God's Children—
Honoring Our Neighbor's Faith 57

Out and About: Our Neighbor Down the Street 61

Worship Service: A Jewish Worship Experience 63

How to Use Faith in Motion

Leader's Guide

Information and Formation

Topic and Key Verse
This Life-to-Bible curriculum starts with important topics for junior highs and goes to God's Word.

Take-Home Learning
The goal for the session is clear.

Younger Youth and This Topic
Find out more about your youth and how they are likely to connect with this concern.

Theology and This Topic
How does Christian faith and tradition help us to understand and deal with the concern?

You and the Scripture
Our being formed as a Christian through Bible reflection and prayer is essential for our teaching.

Transformation

The ultimate goal: Youth will become more fully devoted disciples of Jesus Christ.

Overview Chart
Look here for the big picture of the session. Also note the key activities, just in case time is tight.

Jump Right In!
The opening activity engages youth as they arrive.

Experience It!
Learning activities give youth a common base for making new connections.

Explore Connections
What do the Scriptures have to say? What does this mean for my life? What is a Christian to do?

Take the Challenge
The learnings are not just for Sunday!

Encounter the Holy
Ritual and mystery, prayer and commitment change hearts.

Student Journal and Reproducible Handouts

Life Focus
Topics deal with issues and concerns important to junior high youth.

Spirit Forming
The journal provides practical help and scriptural encouragement.

Group Friendly
Printed Scripture references, discussion questions, and handouts facilitate participation by individuals and small groups.

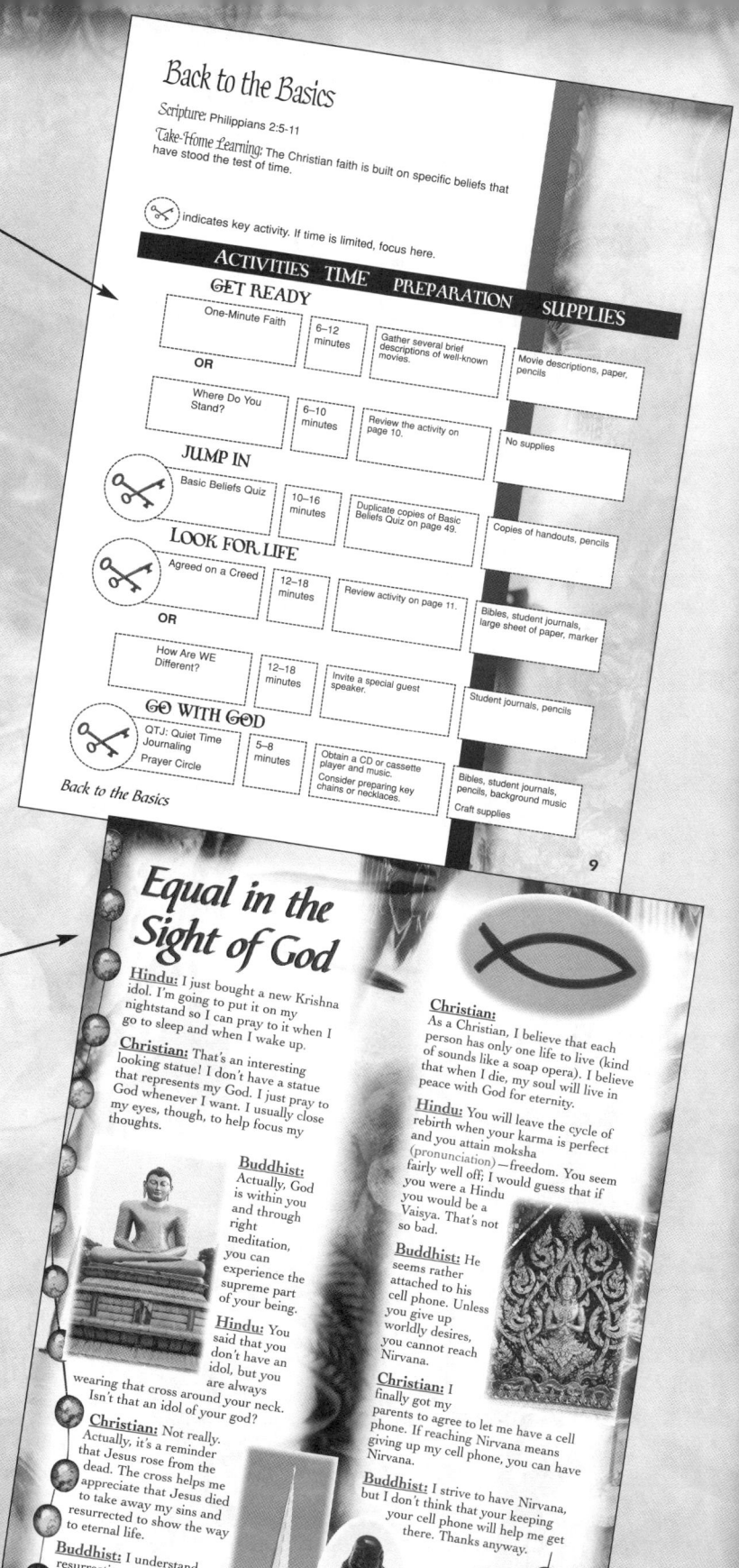

Back to the Basics

Scripture: Philippians 2:5-11

Take-Home Learning: The Christian faith is built on specific beliefs that have stood the test of time.

🔑 indicates key activity. If time is limited, focus here.

ACTIVITIES	TIME	PREPARATION	SUPPLIES
GET READY			
One-Minute Faith	6–12 minutes	Gather several brief descriptions of well-known movies.	Movie descriptions, paper, pencils
OR			
Where Do You Stand?	6–10 minutes	Review the activity on page 10.	No supplies
JUMP IN			
🔑 Basic Beliefs Quiz	10–16 minutes	Duplicate copies of Basic Beliefs Quiz on page 49.	Copies of handouts, pencils
LOOK FOR LIFE			
🔑 Agreed on a Creed	12–18 minutes	Review activity on page 11.	Bibles, student journals, large sheet of paper, marker
OR			
How Are WE Different?	12–18 minutes	Invite a special guest speaker.	Student journals, pencils
GO WITH GOD			
🔑 QTJ: Quiet Time Journaling / Prayer Circle	5–8 minutes	Obtain a CD or cassette player and music. Consider preparing key chains or necklaces.	Bibles, student journals, pencils, background music, Craft supplies

Back to the Basics

Equal in the Sight of God

Hindu: I just bought a new Krishna idol. I'm going to put it on my nightstand so I can pray to it when I go to sleep and when I wake up.

Christian: That's an interesting looking statue! I don't have a statue that represents my God. I just pray to God whenever I want. I usually close my eyes, though, to help focus my thoughts.

Buddhist: Actually, God is within you and through right meditation, you can experience the supreme part of your being.

Hindu: You said that you don't have an idol, but you are always wearing that cross around your neck. Isn't that an idol of your god?

Christian: Not really. Actually, it's a reminder that Jesus rose from the dead. The cross helps me appreciate that Jesus died to take away my sins and resurrected to show the way to eternal life.

Buddhist: I understand resurrection. Each time we die, our soul resurrects and transmigrates into another form.

Christian: As a Christian, I believe that each person has only one life to live (kind of sounds like a soap opera). I believe that when I die, my soul will live in peace with God for eternity.

Hindu: You will leave the cycle of rebirth when your karma is perfect and you attain moksha (pronunciation)—freedom. You seem fairly well off; I would guess that if you were a Hindu you would be a Vaisya. That's not so bad.

Buddhist: He seems rather attached to his cell phone. Unless you give up worldly desires, you cannot reach Nirvana.

Christian: I finally got my parents to agree to let me have a cell phone. If reaching Nirvana means giving up my cell phone, you can have Nirvana.

Buddhist: I strive to have Nirvana, but I don't think that your keeping your cell phone will help me get there. Thanks anyway.

Preparing for This Series

The Purposes of This Study:

Youth hear about other religions and many of them go to school with young persons of other faiths. The purposes of this study are to help youth see value in the Christian faith and claim it as their own while at the same time increasing their understanding and respect for persons of other religions.

Highly Recommended Reading for This Series:

In addition to a world map or globe, encyclopedias, dictionaries of world religions, world almanacs, and other reference materials, check your local library for the following resources and others:

Honoring Our Neighbor's Faith, edited by Robert Buckley Farlee (Augsburg Fortress, © 1999). An overview of thirty-two denominations and major world religions found in the United States.

Relating to People of Other Religions: What Every Christian Needs to Know by M. Thomas Thangaraj (Abingdon Press, © 1997). A thoughtful but brief exploration of several different approaches to interreligious dialogue and Christian perspectives on other faiths.

To the Point: Confronting Youth Issues—Religions, edited by Diana L. Hynson (Abingdon Press, © 1995). A guide to discussing world religions and Christian denominations with youth.

A Visual Treasury of United Methodism (Cokesbury, © 2000). Provides a glimpse of the richness of Christian church history.

Internet Websites:

www.beliefnet.com
www.jewfaq.org
www.hindunet.org
www.adherents.com

www.religioustolerance.org/christ.htm
www.islam.com
www.nandawon.demon.co.uk/vihara/intro00.htm#intro

(At the time of publication, all website addresses were correct and operational. Addresses may change in the future.)

Pictures:

World Religions Poster Series: Five posters depicting five of the world's major religions studied in this series. Available from *www.knowledgeunlimited.com*.

Videos and CD-ROMs:

Most videos on world religions are too long to use in one session, but consider using short clips. Check your local library, educational or religious media center, church library, or local synagogues, mosques, and temples for appropriate videos or CD-ROMs. Consider the following:

- *Faith and Belief: Five Major World Religions* (Knowledge Unlimited, © 1992). A brief video series discussing each of the five major religions studied in this resource. Video segments are 21 minutes and can be used throughout the study. Order from *www.knowledgeunlimited.com*.

- *World Religions* (Delphi Productions, Ltd. © 2002). A video series available at *www.ecufilm.com*. Each video is approximately 20–28 minutes in length.

- *Religions of the World* (Schlessinger Media © 2002). A thirteen-video series; can be purchased as a set and individually at *www.knowledgeunlimited.com* or *www.libraryvideo.com*.

SESSION 1

Back to the Basics

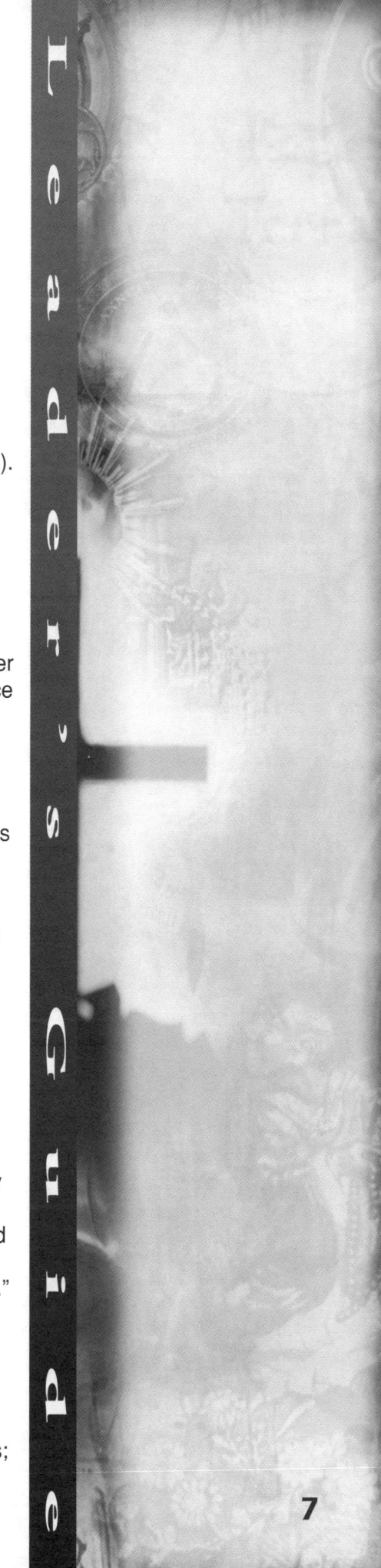

Topic: The Basics of Christian Faith

Scripture: Philippians 2:5-11

Key Verse: "Being found in human form, he humbled himself and became obedient to the point of death—even death on a cross" (Philippians 2:7-8).

Take-Home Learning: The Christian faith is built on specific beliefs that have stood the test of time.

Younger Youth and This Topic

In subjects such as math or English, the knowledge youth gain builds over time as they learn concepts and develop skills. Christian faith and practice are like that to some degree, but they are more complex due to several factors, including:

- One's experience of God is personal and subjective.

- Younger youth are at a developmental stage where they can process everything at a deeper level, resulting in their asking the question, "Why?" about much of what they have learned or believe.

- Most likely, the youth of your church have not grown up learning the same things at the same time about the Christian faith.

Even if you think your youth are well-versed on the basics of Christianity, they may still hold some religious views that are different from traditional Christian faith. Or, they may be curious about why their friends have different views than they do about Jesus, the Bible, the afterlife, and so on. Use this session as a time to help them review (or learn) the basics and begin to develop their own faith creeds.

At this stage in their development, their faith is not likely to be completely based in logic or thought; it's more reasonable to assume their faith is linked with their emotional experiences of God. Developing a group creed is not a way of helping youth form a comprehensive theology, but it is a powerful way of helping them to state, "Here's what we believe right now."

Theology and This Topic

Let's be honest: There is no one right way to express or practice the Christian faith. Each denomination has its own theological distinctiveness;

Back to the Basics

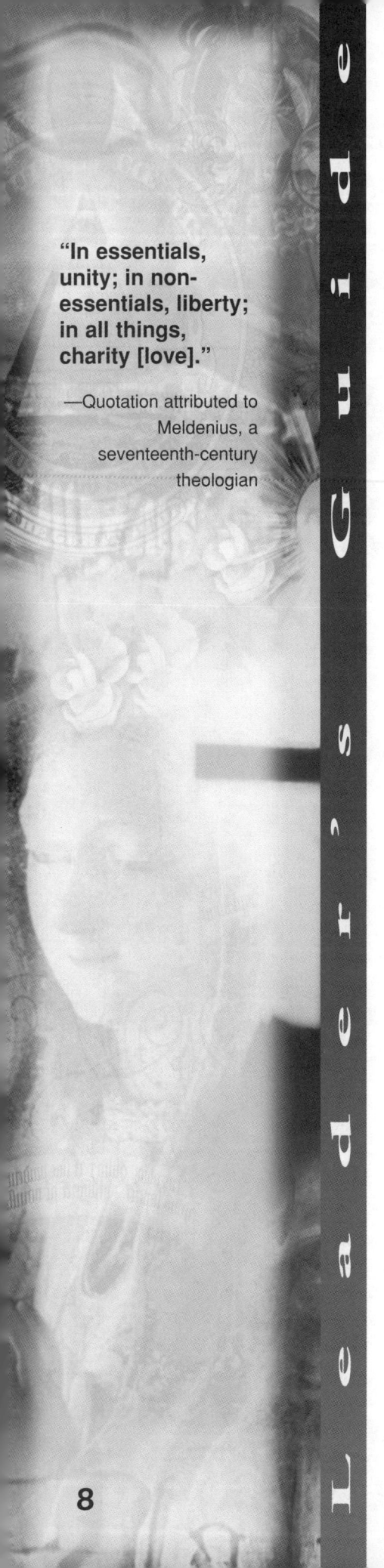

> "In essentials, unity; in non-essentials, liberty; in all things, charity [love]."
>
> —Quotation attributed to Meldenius, a seventeenth-century theologian

theologians hold well-thought-out but often widely differing views, and Scripture does not present only one view of God or Jesus. This fact also holds true for Judaism, Islam, and many other religions of the world. Defining the "basic beliefs" of our faith is not as easy as tract writers might have us believe. So we're faced with a choice. Either we can assert dogmatically that we alone have the truth and others do not, or we can realize that, as Paul said, "Now I know only in part; then I will know fully" (1 Corinthians 13:12).

Defining our basic beliefs is critical to having a faith identity, but we do so knowing that we cannot see the big picture. Our beliefs are like the structure of a house. That is, beliefs help to give shape to everything else we believe and do within that house—and beliefs are vitally important to building a house. Yet, our home is not exactly like that of our neighbor. Our stance toward our neighbor needs to be one of respect, while at the same time we become clearer about the beliefs that make us who we are.

You and the Scripture

- What are key Scriptures on which your faith is built? Look through your Bible, find the verses, and list them here. Refer to them during the session.

- How has your faith changed since you were a younger youth? What brought about those changes?

- Read the Apostles' Creed and the Statement of Faith of the United Church of Canada on page 5 in the student journal. You might also check your church's hymnal or worship book for additional creeds. Which of these means the most to you? Why?

Choosing Jesus: The Real Deal on the Spiritual Menu

Back to the Basics

Scripture: Philippians 2:5-11

Take-Home Learning: The Christian faith is built on specific beliefs that have stood the test of time.

🗝️ indicates key activity. If time is limited, focus here.

ACTIVITIES	TIME	PREPARATION	SUPPLIES
GET READY			
One-Minute Faith	6–12 minutes	Gather several brief descriptions of well-known movies.	Movie descriptions, paper, pencils
OR			
Where Do You Stand?	6–10 minutes	Review the activity on page 10.	No supplies
JUMP IN			
🗝️ Basic Beliefs Quiz	10–16 minutes	Duplicate copies of Basic Beliefs Quiz on page 49.	Copies of handouts, pencils
LOOK FOR LIFE			
🗝️ Agreed on a Creed	12–18 minutes	Review activity on page 11.	Bibles, student journals, large sheet of paper, marker
OR			
How Are WE Different?	12–18 minutes	Invite a special guest speaker.	Student journals, pencils
GO WITH GOD			
🗝️ QTJ: Quiet Time Journaling / Prayer Circle	5–8 minutes	Obtain a CD or cassette player and music. Consider preparing key chains or necklaces.	Bibles, student journals, pencils, background music / Craft supplies

Back to the Basics

GET READY

Provide several descriptions of well-known movies, paper, and pencils.

One-Minute Faith (6–12 minutes)

Before the session, choose several movie descriptions from the "One-Minute Movie" website: *http://www.rinkworks.com/movieaminute*. Or, look in your newspaper listings for a one-sentence summary of current movies. Choose movies that are very well-known or that most of the youth in your group will have seen.

Read aloud the descriptions, then say: "I'd like you to come up with a one-minute description of one of the following: the story of the Bible, the life of Jesus, or what it means to be a Christian."

Pass out paper and pencils. Allow youth a few minutes to work on their one-minute descriptions, then ask for volunteers to read them aloud. (If you think the youth will be shy about reading what they've written, collect the papers and read them anonymously.) It's OK to have fun with this assignment. Some of the one-minute movie descriptions are hilarious!

OR

Where Do You Stand? (6–10 minutes)

Say: "I'm going to read aloud two words or phrases, and I'd like you to choose the one you think best describes Christianity. You may actually want to land somewhere in the middle of each choice, but I'd like you to pick one or the other. Move to the side of the room that represents one of the choices I give you." As you read aloud the choices, point to the side of the room where youth who agree need to move.

Read aloud the first set of choices and direct the youth to move. Ask a few youth to explain why they chose that particular side. Follow the same process for each pair of choices.

- Mystery or Certainty
- Freedom or Rules
- Black and White or Shades of Gray
- Heart or Head
- Flexible or Strict
- One Size Fits All or Custom Fit
- The Only Truth or One Truth Among Many
- Focused on Helping Others or Focused on Saving Souls

JUMP IN

Provide copies of Basic Beliefs Quiz on page 49 and pencils.

Basic Beliefs Quiz (10–16 minutes)

Say: "Most people in the world know very little about what Christians believe. In fact, many Christians aren't that sure. Here's a quick quiz to see how well you know the basic Christian beliefs."

Choosing Jesus: The Real Deal on the Spiritual Menu

Pass out copies of the Basic Beliefs Quiz. You may choose to divide youth into small groups, or, if you think most of the youth are unfamiliar with basic Christian beliefs, you may want to complete the quiz together.

Option: Consider developing the quiz into a game show. Assign teams, ask one question per team, and accept only one answer per group.

After everyone has finished the quiz, ask:

- Which of these beliefs are the essential or most important beliefs of Christians?
- Are beliefs missing from this list?

Agreed on a Creed (12–18 minutes)

Say: "Throughout history, Christians have written and recited creeds that might be considered *CliffsNotes™* versions of the Christian faith. Basically, a creed is a collection of statements indicating what an individual or community believes. One of the earliest creeds is found in the Bible. Let's read together Philippians 2:5-11." Read the Scripture in unison, then ask:

- According to this Scripture, what does Paul believe about Jesus?
- Have you memorized any of the creeds we sometimes say during worship? (If so, allow a volunteer to recite one he or she remembers.)

Say: "The creeds that most people recognize, such as the Nicene Creed and the Apostles' Creed, were both written to clarify what the church held as the true beliefs of Christians. The statements also were a means of stating that some of the beliefs people held as Christian were actually false. In other words, creeds often reflect the concerns and ideas regarding the Christian faith during the time they were written. There also are modern creeds that reflect what particular churches or denominations believe about what it means to be a Christian. Let's read one of these together."

Pass out the student journals and together read or recite the Apostles' Creed (if you didn't recite it earlier) as well as the Statement of Faith of the United Church of Canada (page 5). Then ask:

- What did you like about the second creed?
- Are there phrases with which you disagree or that you don't understand?

Say: "We will begin writing our own group creed this week, and we'll continue to work on it over the next few weeks. Each time we meet, we'll add a statement or two that sums up what we agree on as it relates to the topic. To get started, let's look at the creed starters on page 6 in the student journal. Choose two or three of these creed starters (or make up your own), and list your ideas for what our creed might include. Then, in about three minutes, we'll share our lists, see what we have in common, and if we agree on any of our ideas."

Back to the Basics

Answers to Basic Beliefs Quiz on page 49:
1. C; 2. C; 3. C; 4. C;
5. C; 6. B; 7. C; 8. B;
9. C; 10. C; 11. B;
12. B; 13. B; 14. B;
15. A; 16. A; 17. A;
18. B; 19. A; 20. B; 21. B; 22. C.

Note: These answers are subject to interpretation. "All," for example, may be more accurately termed "most" in some cases. "Some" may be more accurately termed "a few" who are outside the mainline. The point is less about the "Alls" and "Somes" than it is that students recognize the "Nones"!

LOOK FOR LIFE

Provide Bibles, student journals, pencils, large sheet of paper, and marker.

Wait three minutes, then read the statements one at a time, working together to compose a simple sentence that incorporates the ideas from the youth. Write the statement on a large sheet of paper and display it throughout the study. If time is short, remember that you will continue to work on the creed in coming weeks.

Due to the limited time, don't expect youth to produce a creed that will stand the test of time. This is a "snapshot," revealing what the youth believe now, not necessarily what they will always believe. The process of thinking through and writing down their beliefs is important as well as the content that is meaningful to them.

OR

How Are WE Different? (12–18 minutes)

Provide student journals and pencils.

Prior to the session, invite a pastor, layleader, seminary student, or other church official to talk with the group about the unique beliefs, practices, or theological emphases of your denomination. Ask your speaker to prepare a very brief, three-to-four-minute talk including the most important points. If a speaker is unavailable, prepare to present the unique beliefs of your denomination.

After the presentation, discuss any questions youth may have and refer them to page 7 in their student journals to see beliefs Christians share.

QTJ: Quiet Time Journaling (5–8 minutes)

Distribute student journals. Encourage youth to spend a few minutes in silence answering the questions in "A Life in a Comma" on page 4. Play soft music in the background as they work.

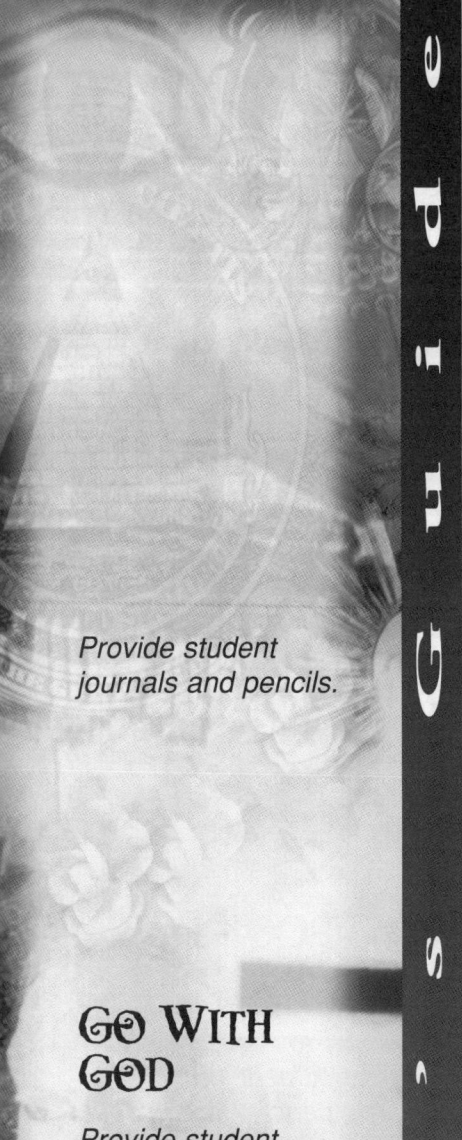

GO WITH GOD

Provide student journals, pencils, CD or cassette player, and soft, background music.

If possible, make a key chain or necklace with a comma on it for each youth. For example, you might use beads with letters and symbols (available at a craft store) in this way: a comma: ",", followed by the name of the youth and another comma: ",".

Read aloud the phrase, *"... born of the virgin Mary, suffered under Pontius Pilate... ."* Then say: "Practically all of Jesus' life is represented by the comma in this phrase of the creed! But that 'life in a comma' has changed the world. It's that life we are called to imitate as Christians."

Gather youth into a prayer circle. If you have time, ask: "What were qualities that people observed in Jesus during his ministry on earth?" (*Possible answers are: compassionate, healer, good teacher, prophet, and so forth.*) "Are they the same qualities people see in Jesus today?"

Say: "These are just a few of the characteristics and qualities we see in Jesus that made his life count for so much. What would you like your life to stand for, and what would you like people to see in you?" (*Possible suggestions are a good friend, a faithful disciple, helpful, and so forth.*)

Close with prayer, giving thanks for the life and teachings of Jesus and asking for God's help in following Jesus' teachings.

Choosing Jesus: The Real Deal on the Spiritual Menu

SESSION 2

Beyond Wings and Halos— A Look at Angels in the Bible

Topic: Helping Youth Differentiate Between Biblical and Popular Understandings of Angels

Scripture: Exodus 3:1-10; 23:20-25; 24:3; Judges 13:1, 24; 2 Kings 19:1-8; Psalm 91:9-11; Matthew 1:18-25; Luke 1:5-38; Acts 5:17-21a; 8:25-38; Hebrews 13:2

Key Verse: "Do not neglect to show hospitality to strangers, for by doing that some have entertained angels without knowing it" (Hebrews 13:2).

Take-Home Learning: When it comes to angels in the Bible, the message is far more important than the messenger.

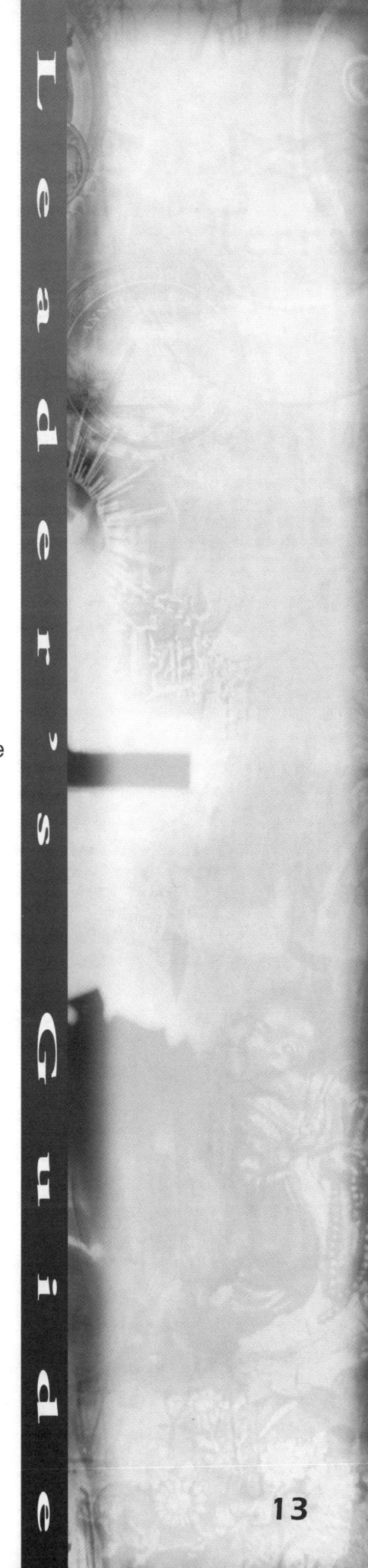

Younger Youth and This Topic

Chances are good that many of the youth in your church have portrayed angels in a childhood Christmas pageant, complete with tinsel halos and white robes. Many probably have seen dozens of angel characters in shows on television such as *Touched by an Angel* or *Angel*.

If you were to ask your group how many of them believe in angels, you'd learn that most of them do. However, most of their images and ideas about angels come from popular culture and not the Bible. Even those who know the Bible well may be familiar only with the angels of the Gospels and perhaps the Book of Revelation.

The danger for many of us is that we can become fixated on the personal nature (such as guardian angels) or the form (beautiful creatures with robes, wings, and halos) of angels and overlook their function and messages in the Bible. Your task is to help youth see that we should neither worship angels nor disregard them as merely legend. Focus attention on the middle ground, learning from the messages delivered by angels in the Scriptures.

Beyond Wings and Halos—A Look at Angels in the Bible

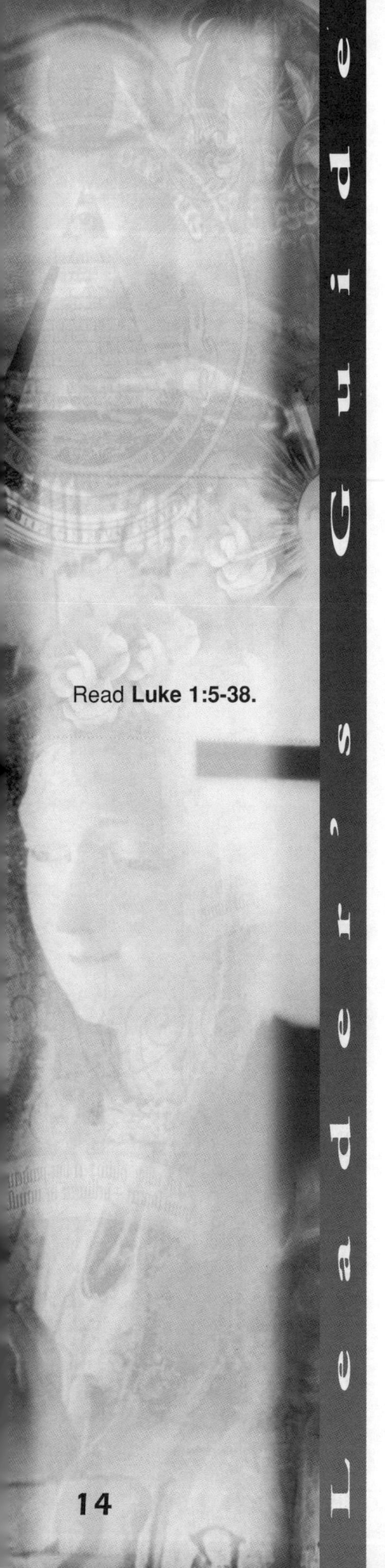

Theology and This Topic

Three understandings about angels in the Bible are significant:

1. The Israelites' concept and understanding of angels developed over time. This development grew from interactions with other cultures and religions, increased interest in and speculation about all things supernatural, and an increase in the understanding of God as transcendent and separate from us.

2. Bible writers used the concept of angels to help readers understand the message. The message is always more important than the messenger. Angels are generally indistinguishable from ordinary people in the Bible except for the messages they deliver—messages from God.

3. Frequently, the messages angels deliver are about justice and action. Often angels are portrayed as holders of great knowledge and discernment who give reassurance, commission individuals to particular tasks, and speak God's Word to the prophets.

You and the Scripture

Re-read the beginning of the Christmas story in Luke 1:5-38. Is it the appearance of the angel or the message that is frightening in this story?

Although popular interest in angels was at its peak a few years ago, speculation about these supernatural beings is still strong. In biblical times, interest in angels had a direct connection to the people's views of God. As individuals experienced God as more transcendent (different or distant) and less immanent (similar or close), they had a need for divine mediators. The same is likely true today: When people emphasize the holiness and greatness of God, which puts God "watching us—from a distance," interest in angels usually increases. For some individuals, thinking about angels is a way of experiencing God more personally.

- What do you believe about angels? How did you arrive at those beliefs?

- How important are angels to your faith and understanding of God?

- How comfortable are you when talking with people about angels?

- To what degree can you accept the beliefs of people who have different understandings of angels than your own? What about youth who don't believe in angels at all?

Read **Luke 1:5-38.**

Choosing Jesus: The Real Deal on the Spiritual Menu

Beyond Wings and Halos—
A Look at Angels in the Bible

Scripture: Exodus 3:1-10; 23:20-25; 24:3; Judges 13:1, 24; 1 Kings 19:1-8; Psalm 91:9-11; Matthew 1:18-25; Acts 5:17-21a; 8:25-38; Hebrews 13:2

Take-Home Learning: When it comes to angels in the Bible, the message is far more important than the messenger.

🗝 indicates key activity. If time is limited, focus here.

ACTIVITY	TIME	PREPARATION	SUPPLIES

GET READY

| An "Angelic" Visitor | 10–15 minutes | Plan to serve simple snacks. Enlist a person to roleplay an angel. | Snacks, costume for "angel" |

OR

| No Fear Here | 4–8 minutes | Review No Fear Here activity on page 16. | No supplies |

JUMP IN

🗝 | Pictures of Angels or Our Own Angel Stories | 8–10 minutes / 2–4 minutes | Label a large sheet of paper. See page 17. | Sheets of individual and large paper, markers, tape |

LOOK FOR LIFE

🗝 | Angel Encounters | 10–14 minutes | Duplicate copies of Encounters of Another Kind on page 50. | Copies of handouts, pencils |

GO WITH GOD

| Continue the Creed | 5–8 minutes | Post the creed begun in last week's session. | Markers |

OR

🗝 | QTJ: Quiet Time Journaling / Closing Prayer | 5–7 minutes | Plan to play soft, background music while youth work. | Bibles, student journals, pencils, CD or cassette player, background music |

Beyond Wings and Halos—A Look at Angels in the Bible

GET READY

Provide snacks.

Prior to the session, ask a person from your church (someone the youth don't know very well) to visit the group as an "angel" and to deliver the speech provided in the activity. Help him or her to dress the part using a Christmas costume or a choir robe. Hide the "angel" until time for the proclamation. Direct the "angel" to burst into the room, deliver the speech, and then quickly leave.

If you choose to "canvas the church," alert the other Sunday school classes about the potential disruption and gain their permission.

An "Angelic" Visitor (10–15 minutes)

As the youth arrive, spend a few minutes simply chatting, eating snacks, and visiting. Observe their reactions when the "angel" bursts in and makes the following proclamation:

"Behold, I bring you good news. God has chosen you for a special task. In this very city, many people are in need. Together, your congregation can touch the lives of others by sharing individual skills and resources! Do not be afraid, but go forth from this place and serve the Lord your God."

Say: "I don't know about you, but when God sends a messenger my way, I'm inclined to do what that messenger says." Ask:

- To what needs do you think the angel might have been referring?
- What can we do immediately to address these needs?

Spend a minute or two brainstorming ideas you can accomplish quickly. For example, you might visit other groups, share the angel's message, and receive an offering. Or, you could enlist people for a weekend tour of a homeless shelter in your area. If possible, divide youth into small groups and canvas the church as quickly as possible.

Once you've returned to your meeting room, debrief the experience of sharing the angel's message. Ask:

- What was your first reaction when I said we needed to go and do what the angel said?
- Of what, if anything, were you afraid?

OR

No Fear Here (4–8 minutes)

Engage the arriving students in conversation using this imaginary scenario:

> A messenger you don't know unexpectedly appears and tells you that God wants you to do something or go somewhere that seems radical to you.

- Would you follow the messenger's instructions?
- What attitudes or actions might keep you from following the messenger's instructions?
- What attitudes or actions might convince you to do what is asked?

Choosing Jesus: The Real Deal on the Spiritual Menu

Pictures of Angels (8–10 minutes)

Handout sheets of paper and markers to individuals or have two or three students gather around a large sheet of paper. Ask them to draw one or more angels and list words or phrases that describe angels and what they do.

While the youth are drawing, post a large sheet of paper and draw a vertical line down the center. Label the left side, *Our Images of Angels;* label the right side, *Where Angels Come From.*

When most youth are finished with their pictures and descriptions, ask them to "popcorn" (yell out randomly) the elements they have included. List their responses on the chart. Then ask:

- Where do you think these ideas come from? *(Some suggestions are TV, movies, art, Christmas decorations.)*

Now invite youth to look at the Bible's depiction of angels.

OR

Our Own Angel Stories (2–4 minutes)

A few people do have stories of angels in their lives. If you are aware of such persons in your church, invite them to talk with your youth about the experiences. Then ask if any of the youth have stories to share.

Pass out student journals. Refer to the key Scripture, Hebrews 13:2, and direct students to answer the questions on page 8. Review the questions together, discussing the relationship between hospitality and angels.

Angel Encounters (10–14 minutes)

Pass out pencils and copies of Encounters of Another Kind on page 50.

Say: "We're going to take a look at a few Bible people and their encounters with angels."

Divide youth into pairs or teams of three or four and assign each team two or three of the Scripture passages. Instruct the youth to summarize the situations, the angels' messages, the Bible persons' reactions, and how the person or people responded. Allow approximately eight minutes for work, then regroup and ask teams to report their answers.

Then ask:

- As you read these stories and listened to all the teams' answers, what did you discover the answers had in common?
- What do angels do?

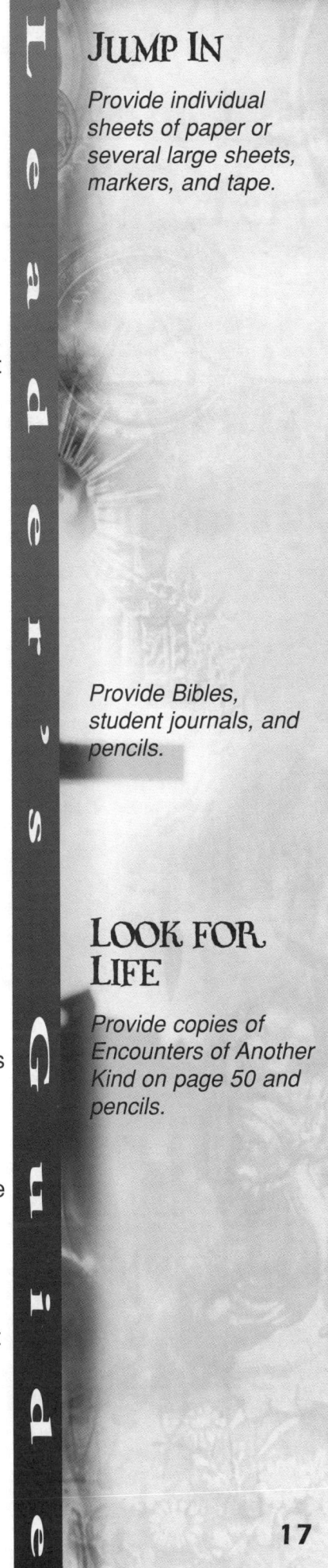

Beyond Wings and Halos—A Look at Angels in the Bible

JUMP IN

Provide individual sheets of paper or several large sheets, markers, and tape.

Provide Bibles, student journals, and pencils.

LOOK FOR LIFE

Provide copies of Encounters of Another Kind on page 50 and pencils.

GO WITH GOD

Provide Bibles, student journals, pencils, CD or cassette player, and soft, background music.

Remember to post the creed begun during last week's session.

Continue the Creed (5–8 minutes)

Remind youth about the group creed they began during the last session. Ask:

- Is there a statement based on today's topic that you would like to add to our creed?

Spend a few minutes brainstorming ideas, refining the statement, and adding to the group creed. Then, together, read the creed-in-progress to close your session.

QTJ: Quiet Time Journaling (5–7 minutes)

Distribute student journals and pencils. Allow youth to spend five minutes in silence answering the questions on pages 10–11. Play soft, background music while they work.

Close by reading aloud Psalm 91:9-11. Emphasize that God's angels watch over those who love God.

Choosing Jesus: The Real Deal on the Spiritual Menu

SESSION 3

Misled and Misleading: Cults

Topic: Recognizing Cults and Groups With Cult-like Behavior

Scripture: Deuteronomy 4:1-2; Psalm 119:122; Matthew 16:13-17; John 14:26; Romans 8:3; Galatians 5:18-23; Ephesians 1:7-8a; 2:8; Colossians 2:6-8,18-19; 2 Timothy 1:8-9a; 3:14-17; 1 Peter 4:10; 1 John 4:9

Key Verse: "Then he said to them all, 'If any want to become my followers, let them deny themselves and take up their cross daily and follow me'" (Luke 9:23).

Take-Home Learning: Be careful of those who encourage you not to think about your faith.

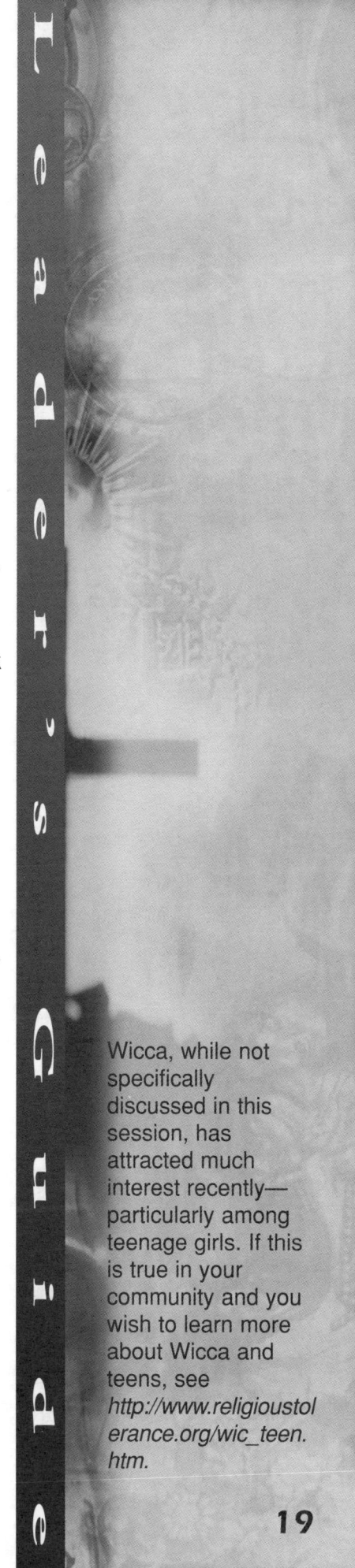

Younger Youth and This Topic

Interest in cults and cult-like practices among youth varies greatly from region to region. Some youth in your town might be interested in Wicca, a Neo-Pagan religion that is rooted in feminine images and a connection to nature. Other youth might be attracted to Satanism or a fascination with the occult as a result of seeing this religion portrayed on television or in the movies. Still others might be attracted to a popular youth group in your town which boasts an ultra-charismatic leader and practices what you believe to be questionable and objectionable recruitment techniques.

If there is evidence in your community that youth are drawn to a group that you or your church consider to be a cult, ask yourself these questions:

- Are we creating a climate and systems that welcome and connect youth within the church?

- Are we touching the deep spiritual needs of youth?

- Are we teaching Christian belief without communicating exclusion, judgment, and elitism?

- Are we engaging youth meaningfully in the practices of the faith— not just the habit?[1]

Wicca, while not specifically discussed in this session, has attracted much interest recently— particularly among teenage girls. If this is true in your community and you wish to learn more about Wicca and teens, see http://www.religioustolerance.org/wic_teen.htm.

Misled and Misleading: Cults

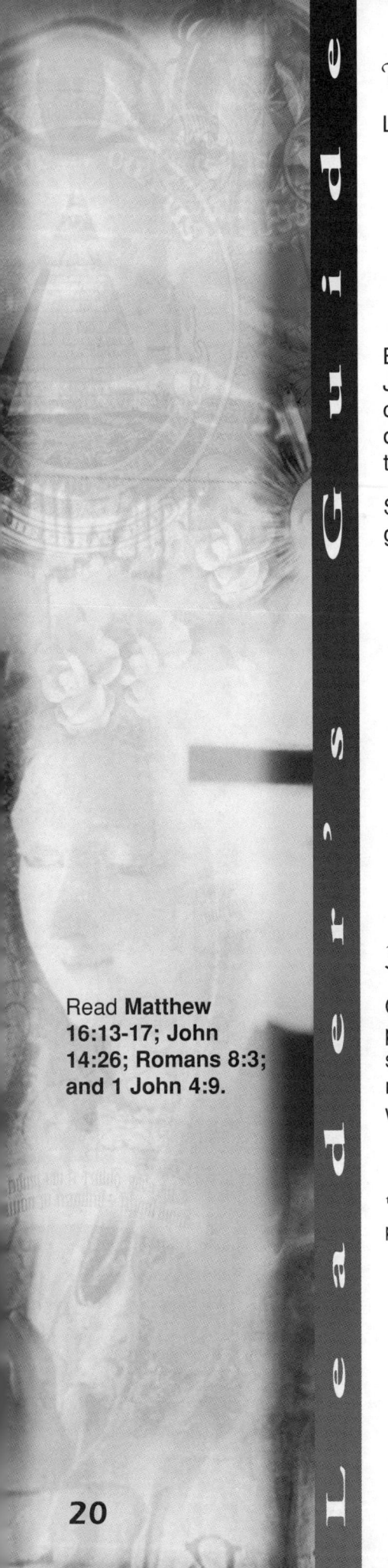

Theology and This Topic

Let's look at some definitions so we're all on the same page:

- A *religion* is an organized faith that is widely accepted and has existed for a long period of time.
- A *sect* is a group that splits from a religion or a church.
- A *cult* is a group with new expressions of religious practice and belief.

By this definition, initially Judaism was a new cult and Christianity was a Jewish sect. It should be clear that part of the challenge in critiquing contemporary cults or sects is that the major religions of the world were once considered new and threatening to the established faiths of their time.

Several behaviors serve as warning signs that a particular religious group is dangerous or unhealthy. Beware of a group when they …

- use unprincipled means to recruit new members. For example, Christians should not be in the business of actively "stealing" members from other churches.
- use manipulation and deter critical thinking. Youth should not have to check their brains at the door of any groups in which they participate.
- use pressure to break apart family unity. Youth should not have to choose between faith and family.
- use the leader's authority inappropriately. For example, youth groups should not revolve around one charismatic youth leader.

You and the Scripture

Quite a few Scriptures are included in the "Three Questions" activity on page 51. Take time to carefully read and study these verses. Use a study Bible to help you understand any passages that are unclear. Make notes regarding insights you want to remember and may want to share with your youth.

Read **Matthew 16:13-17; John 14:26; Romans 8:3; and 1 John 4:9.**

---

[1] Reprinted from "What's the Attraction?" in *YouthNet*, Volume VII: No. 2, Spring, 2000; page 3. Used by permission.

Choosing Jesus: The Real Deal on the Spiritual Menu

Misled and Misleading: Cults

Scripture: Deuteronomy 4:1-2; Psalm 119:122; Matthew 16:13-17; John 14:26; Romans 8:3; Galatians 5:18-23; Ephesians 1:7-8a; 2:8; Colossians 2:6-8,18-19; 2 Timothy 1:8-9a; 3:14-17; 1 Peter 4:10; 1 John 4:9

Take-Home Learning: Be careful of those who encourage you not to think about your faith.

🗝 indicates key activity. If time is limited, focus here.

ACTIVITY	TIME	PREPARATION	SUPPLIES
GET READY			
www.ask-a-guru.com	8–10 minutes	Review activity on page 22.	Index cards, pencils
JUMP IN			
🗝 It's Counterfeit	6–8 minutes	Cut out "fake" dollar bills. Provide real dollar bills if possible.	Dollar bills, paper, scissors
OR			
Distorting the Truth	6–8 minutes	Create a distorted picture using a computer.	Computer-generated picture, large sheet of paper, marker
LOOK FOR LIFE			
🗝 Three Questions	12–15 minutes	Duplicate copies of Three Questions on page 51.	Copies of handout, Bibles, pencils
OR			
Top Ten Signs	5–7 minutes	Review activity on page 24.	Student journals
GO WITH GOD			
🗝 QTJ: Quiet Time Journaling / Continue the Creed	6–10 minutes / 4–8 minutes	Display creed begun in session one.	Bibles, student journals, pencils, CD or cassette player, background music

Misled and Misleading: Cults

GET READY

Provide index cards and pencils.

JUMP IN

Provide scissors, dollar bills, if possible, and "fake" dollar bills cut from paper.

Prior to the session, locate paper which has a texture similar to paper money. Cut as many "fake" paper bills as you expect youth. Also provide "real" dollar bills if possible.

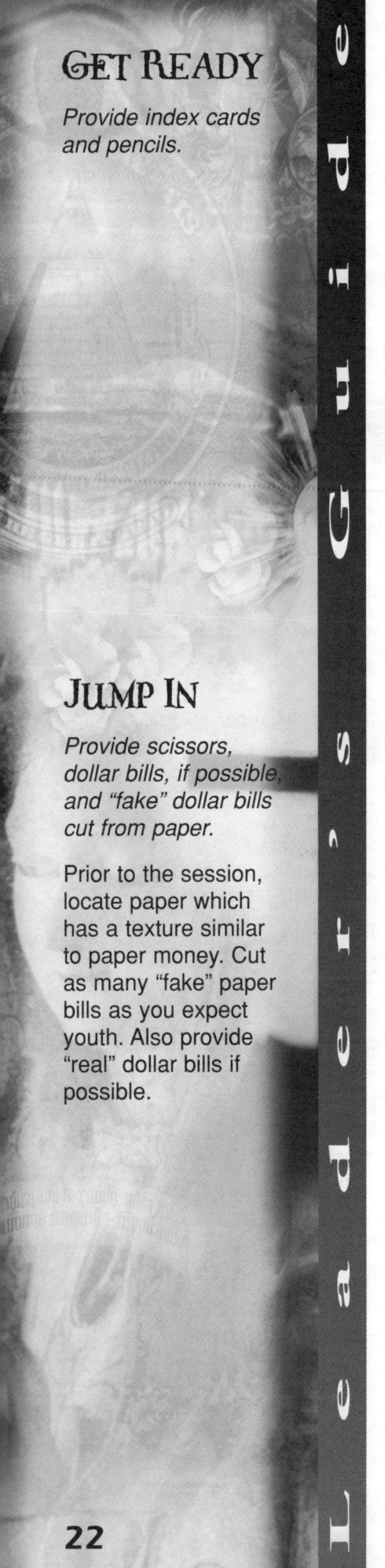

WWW.ASK-A-GURU.COM (8–10 minutes)

Pair up students as they arrive and give each pair two or three index cards and pencils. Direct them to compose a question that they might ask in the chat room of a spiritual website that offers experts to answer questions. The questions can be serious or humorous, and pairs should write one question per card. If youth have difficulty thinking of a question, suggest the following: What is the meaning of life? What happens when I die? Does God have a sense of humor?

After everyone has arrived and all the pairs have submitted at least one question, shuffle the cards, redistribute, and give each pair one new card.

Say: "Now I'd like you to pretend that you are the spiritual guru answering questions at that website. Make up an answer which seems believable yet vague. In other words, don't answer the question exactly, but give advice that could be true."

When all of the questions have been answered, collect them and read aloud to the groups, enjoying a few laughs along the way.

It's Counterfeit (6–8 minutes)

Blindfold the youth, or ask everyone to close their eyes. Say: "I'm going to place a piece of paper in your hands. With your eyes closed, I want you to feel the paper and tell me what you think it is."

Pass out the fake paper bills and ask: "What did I give you? How sure are you?"

Now tell the youth to place the fake bills on their laps. Explain that you will pass out additional pieces of paper for them to feel. This time, if possible, give everyone a real dollar bill. Ask: "What did I give you this time? How sure are you?"

Direct youth to remove their blindfolds or open their eyes and see if they guessed correctly. Collect the bills and blindfolds.

- If you guessed correctly which piece of paper was the genuine dollar bill, how did you know? *(Because we've handled money a lot; because it felt more like money than the first one.)*

- Since counterfeit money is designed to look just like the real thing, how do you think you would be able to spot fake money? *(By feeling it, by comparing it to the original, by looking for the unique security features, and so on.)*

Say: "Bank tellers learn how to spot fake money by handling real money repeatedly until they have memorized the feel and texture of an authentic paper bill. Then when they touch a fake bill, they know it instantly." Ask:

Choosing Jesus: The Real Deal on the Spiritual Menu

- How is the ability of bank tellers to spot a fake bill similar to the ability of Christians to recognize a cult? (*They know the real thing so well that anything else seems wrong; they know the true beliefs of the Christian church.*)

- What do you remember from our discussion in session one about the basic beliefs of Christianity? (If youth are slow to remember, summarize the main points.)

OR

Distorting the Truth (6–8 minutes)

Before the session, use a computer graphics program to manipulate a picture of something or someone that everyone would recognize—a celebrity, a famous painting, a building in your town, and so on. Distort the picture so that it remains recognizable but is clearly warped. If you don't have a computer program with this capability, enlist help from one of the youth in your church.

Pass around the picture, giving everyone an opportunity to look at it. Then ask: "What's wrong with this picture? Why is it still recognizable?"

Say: "Just as I distorted this picture, some groups distort the Christian message and change it to suit their purposes." Then ask, "What are some ways you would be able to tell if a group or leader were giving you false information or attempting to lead you away from Christianity?" (*By studying and memorizing the Bible, by comparing the suspected false teachings to Jesus' teachings.*)

Option: Design a warped mirror by placing aluminum foil over a slightly curved piece of board or cardboard.

Provide a computer-generated, distorted picture.

Three Questions (12–15 minutes)

Pass out copies of Three Questions on page 51, pencils, and Bibles. Divide the group into small teams of two or three.

Say: "There are three easy questions you can ask about a group to determine if it is a cult or if the group is distorting the Christian message. First, what do they say about who Jesus was/is? Second, what do they believe about the authority of the Bible? Third, what do they teach about grace and doing good works?

"I'd like you to read the Scripture passages on the handout and determine which of the choices listed under these questions can be supported by the Bible. Then decide as a team which answer or answers represent what Christians believe to be the truth."

Assign each team one of the sections; ask each team to choose one person to report answers to the large group. If there are disagreements during the reports, read the Scriptures and discuss.

LOOK FOR LIFE

Provide copies of Three Questions on page 51, Bibles, and pencils.

Misled and Misleading: Cults

Provide student journals.

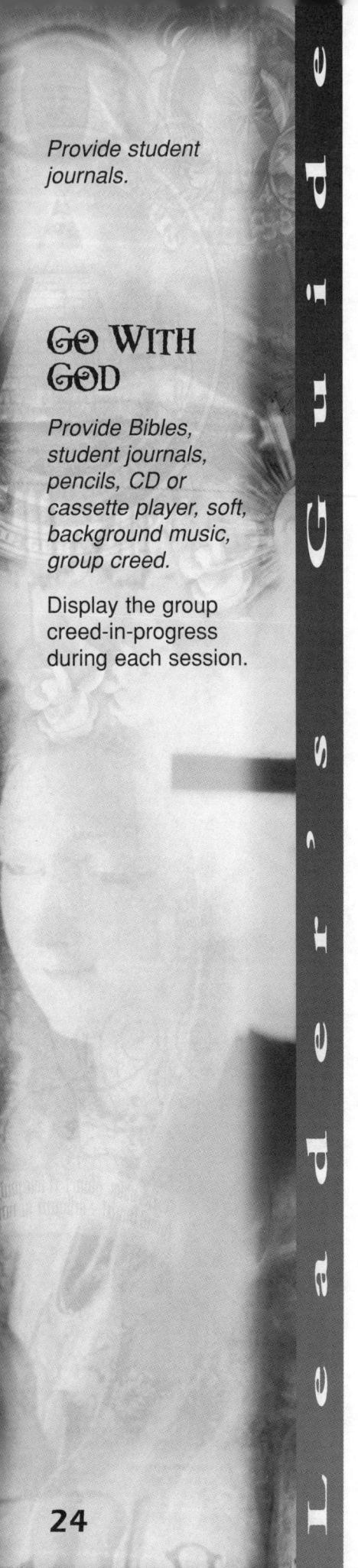

GO WITH GOD

Provide Bibles, student journals, pencils, CD or cassette player, soft, background music, group creed.

Display the group creed-in-progress during each session.

Top Ten Signs (5–7 minutes)

Have fun with this one! Ask for volunteers to read each of the Top Ten Warning Signs on page 13 in the student journal. Stop after reading the list and ask students to come up with some serious advice based on the statements that they would give to a friend who is being influenced toward a cult.

QTJ: Quiet Time Journaling (6–10 minutes)

Pass out student journals. Allow youth five minutes to read "Who Are You Following?" on page 14 and to answer questions. Play soft music in the background while they work.

Close by reading aloud Colossians 2:18-19 from *The Message*:

"Don't tolerate people who try to run your life, ordering you to bow and scrape, insisting that you join their obsession with angels and that you seek out visions. They are a lot of hot air, that's all they are. They're completely out of touch with the source of life, Christ, who puts us together in one piece, whose very breath and blood flow through us. He is the Head and we are the body. We can grow up healthy in God only as he nourishes us."

Continue the Creed (4–8 minutes)

Call attention to the group creed displayed in the meeting room. Ask if there is a statement based on today's topic that they would like to add to the group creed. Work together to refine the statement, then add it to the chart. Read aloud the new creed to close the session.

Choosing Jesus: The Real Deal on the Spiritual Menu

SESSION 4

Children of the One God: Judaism and Islam

Topic: The Basics of Judaism and Islam

Scripture: Exodus 20:1-2; Deuteronomy 6:4-5; Luke 4:16-21

Key Verse: "Hear, O Israel: The LORD is our God, the LORD alone" (Deuteronomy 6:4).

Take-Home Learning: There is one God, and our God is a God who loves diversity.

Younger Youth and This Topic

Unless your town is culturally diverse, odds are good that the majority of the understandings and impressions your youth have of Judaism or Islam come from television news, war scenes from movies, or stereotyped characters on sitcoms. In a post-September 11 world, all of us need to understand these two significant world religions. Judaism isn't just the faith practiced in a land torn by violence; it's also a vital world religion that provided the basis for Christianity. Islam isn't a religion made up of terrorists who wish to destroy America; it's a worldwide religion that is growing faster than Christianity because people find great meaning in its teachings. Christian congregations need to learn about these members of our global community.

The difficulty—even in culturally diverse communities—is that we rarely have the opportunity to dialogue with members of other faiths. Without the ability to get to know one another in meaningful ways, our youth often have only the media to shape their opinions about Jews and Muslims. Use this session as an introduction to these two world religions—but don't stop there. Plan to follow up with trips, cultural events, or jointly planned gatherings with members of a local synagogue or mosque.

Theology and This Topic

Most of our difficulties related to people of other faiths arise out of practical circumstances: What should I do when I'm invited to a Jewish wedding? How should I feel about the increase in violence against Muslims after September 11? My Buddhist coworker seems sincere in his faith, and he practices his religion more faithfully than I practice mine.

Children of the One God: Judaism and Islam

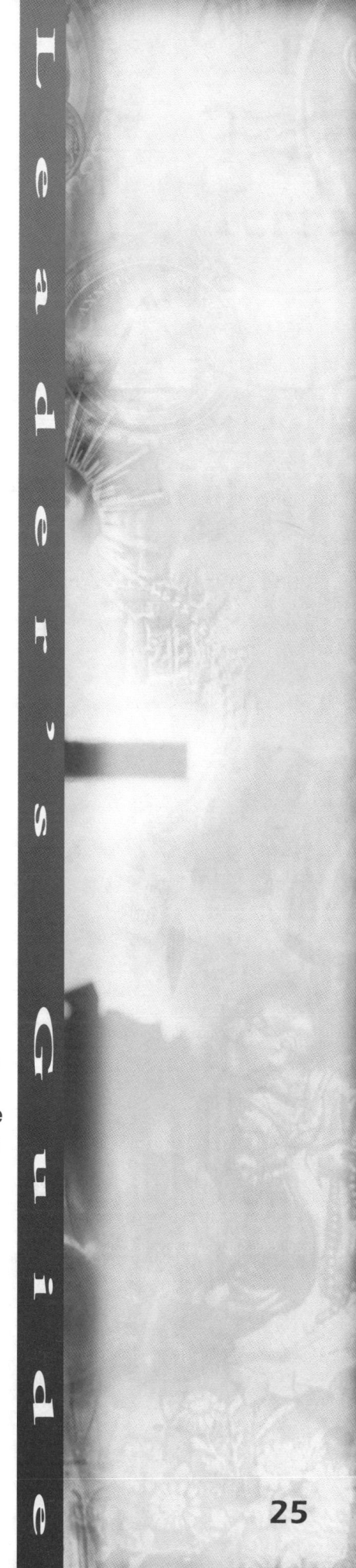

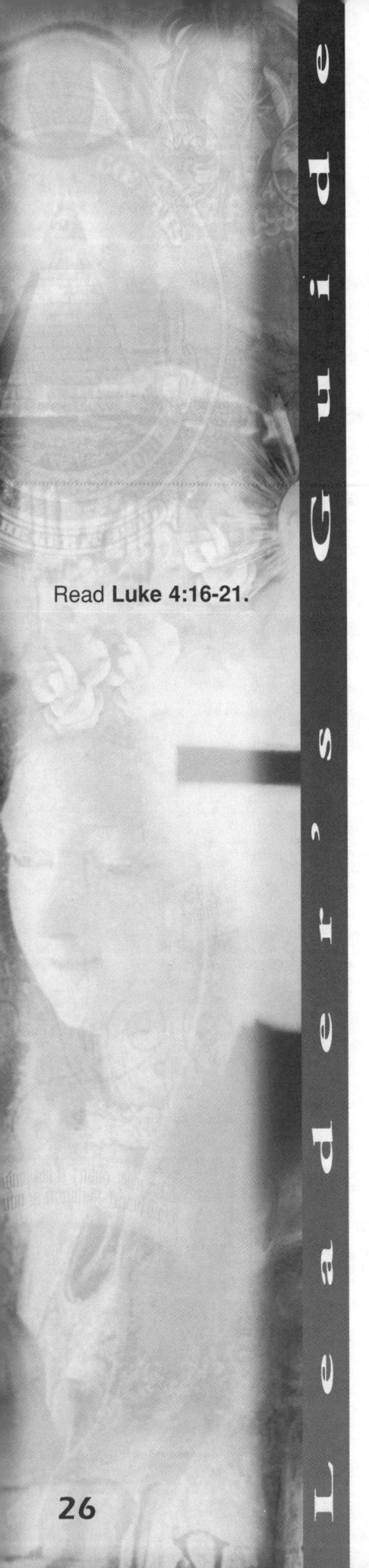

How can I tell him I think he's misguided? Questions such as these cause us to realize the importance of dialogue, and that we can begin to share our faith with integrity only when we are invested in it.

Many books have been written to help people relate to those of different faiths and to approach interreligious dialogue. The issues are extremely complex, and Christian denominations differ on their understandings of how God is revealed within other faiths. In a world that is increasingly diverse and interconnected, we must learn to respect and appreciate one another's faith traditions. Out of that respect may come honest dialogue about our similarities and differences, perhaps resulting in true transformation by those involved.

Despite our many differences, Jews, Muslims, and Christians are all monotheistic—not polytheistic—religions. Our joint conviction is that one God oversees the cosmos, and all other gods are false.

You and the Scripture

Read **Luke 4:16-21.**

The Hebrew Scriptures (Torah) that were a part of Jesus' life are ones that both Jews and Christians claim. The Koran (Qur'an) also testifies to the integrity of the Jewish Torah and the Christian Gospels, and Muslims are encouraged to read and uphold the teachings of these sacred writings.

However, many Christians possess little knowledge of the Scriptures that Jesus knew and that shaped his life and ministry. Our common term for them—the Old Testament—can imply that we should ignore them in favor of the New (and, we assume, improved) Testament.

Reflect on your own understanding of Scripture. Do you …

- see the stories of the Hebrew Bible (the Old Testament) as less likely to have happened than the stories of the New Testament?

- like both parts equally? give the New Testament most of your attention and study? find yourself quoting or teaching only from the New Testament?

- turn only to certain parts of the Hebrew Bible (such as the Psalms or Proverbs) for inspiration and guidance?

- use the Hebrew Bible only to "prove" that segments of the New Testament are true?

If you find that your understanding of the Hebrew Bible is deficient, commit to study it during the next year. Enroll in a Disciple Bible Study group, attend a local college class, or read a good book focused on the Bible. This spiritual discipline will help you to know the mind of Christ!

Choosing Jesus: The Real Deal on the Spiritual Menu

Children of the One God: Judaism and Islam

Scripture: Exodus 20:1-2; Deuteronomy 6:4-5; Luke 4:16-21

Take-Home Learning: There is one God, and our God is a God who loves diversity.

🗝 indicates key activity. If time is limited, focus here.

ACTIVITY	TIME	PREPARATION	SUPPLIES
GET READY			
Where in the World Are They?	10–14 minutes	Obtain a world map or globe. Prepare color chart. Duplicate Where in the World Are They? (page 52).	World map or globe, stick-on dots, copies of handout, large sheet of paper, markers
OR			
Stuck in My Head	5–7 minutes	Prepare three charts with religion titles.	Several packs of sticky notes, three large sheets of paper, markers
JUMP IN			
Begin the Dialogue	15–18 minutes	Invite a member of the Jewish or Muslim community to visit and explain basic beliefs.	No supplies
OR			
🗝 Faith in Focus	15–20 minutes	Duplicate copies of Three Related Religions on page 53. Collect study resources.	Study resources, large sheets of paper, markers, copies of handout
LOOK FOR LIFE			
🗝 Choosing Jesus	15–18 minutes	Review activity on page 29.	No supplies
GO WITH GOD			
🗝 QTJ: Quiet Time Journaling / Continue the Creed	6–8 minutes / 4–8 minutes	Display the group creed worked on during each session.	Bibles, student journals, pencils, CD or cassette player, background music

Children of the One God: Judaism and Islam

GET READY

Provide a recent world map (wall size) or globe, stick-on dots in six different colors (large enough to write a number on), copies of Where in the World Are They? (page 52), a large sheet of paper, and markers.

Before the session, write on a large piece of paper the assigned color of dot for each religion.

If you choose not to do this activity, consider using a religious beliefs chart in an encyclopedia. See also www.adherents.com for more information.

—Statistics used in Where in the World Are They? are based on information from the *New York Times 2001 Almanac.*

Provide several pads of sticky notes, markers, and three large sheets of paper.

Before the session, hang three large sheets of paper. Label one *Judaism,* one *Islam,* and one *We're not sure.*

JUMP IN

Invite a member of the Jewish or Muslim community to visit

28

Leader's Guide

Where in the World Are They? (10–14 minutes)

Pass out copies of Where In the World Are They? on page 52. Say: "We're going to begin looking at some of the other major religions of the world. First, we want to get a sense of where these religions are most commonly practiced."

Divide the group into small teams and assign each team one or two sections of the handout. Then say: "For each country listed on the handout, I'd like you to write on the stickers the percentage of people who practice that faith. Then place that sticker on the proper country on the map. Only place the sticker from the religion with the greatest percentage in a particular country on the map."

Allow several minutes for youth to work, then reassemble teams. Ask:

- On what continents is Christianity most common? Judaism? Islam? Buddhism? Hinduism?

- Which religion would you guess is growing the fastest in the United States? (*Islam*) Why do you think this is happening? (*Many immigrants are coming to the United States from the Middle East; Islam is expanding rapidly in African-American communities.*)

- How do you feel knowing that Christianity is no longer the fastest-growing religion in the United States or in many other countries?

OR

Stuck in My Head (5–7 minutes)

Place a supply of sticky notes and markers on each table. As youth arrive, point out the charts and ask them to write a fact they know, a feeling or impression, or a question they'd like to have answered about these two religions. Suggest they write using large letters so the notes can be read by others. Encourage them to be honest. When they finish writing their notes, tell them to stick them on the appropriate charts.

After everyone has arrived and you have several questions, facts, and impressions, read them to the group; ask for clarification or explanation if necessary. If you or anyone else questions the validity of a question or comment, move it to the chart labeled, *We're not sure*.

When appropriate, use the notes as a springboard for discussion. In particular, you may wish to dialogue about issues that indicate stereotypes and fears related to members of the two faiths as well as to the events of September 11.

Begin the Dialogue (15–18 minutes)

If you've been able to enlist a visitor, introduce him or her at this time. Ask the visitor to speak for five to seven minutes and then allow time for questions from the youth. Here are some suggested questions:

Choosing Jesus: The Real Deal on the Spiritual Menu

- What is the name you most often use to address God and why?
- What is your impression of Christians and Christianity?
- What does your faith believe about Jesus?
- What can we do to increase understanding between the members of our two faiths?

OR

Faith in Focus (15–20 minutes)

Divide youth into three teams. Provide each team a copy of Three Related Religions on page 53 as well as encyclopedias, books, and dictionaries of world religions, markers, and paper. Assign each team a world religion to research: Christianity, Judaism, or Islam. Explain that teams will have about seven minutes to research the religion for a special news report during a nightly news show. The teams are to prepare in these areas:

View of God	Sacred writings
View of history	Unique or important beliefs
View of Jesus	

Suggest they use large sheets of paper to create visual aids for their presentations and keep their reports at two and three minutes each.

After adequate work time, call for team reports. Ask one team member to present information as a news reporter while you act as a moderator, tying together the information. Call for reports in the order the religions were developed: Judaism, Christianity, Islam.

Choosing Jesus (15–18 minutes)

Divide youth into groups of three with one person from each of the three Faith in Focus teams. Have youth play the roles of religious members for the group they were in (Christian, Jew, and Muslim). Ask them to discuss their religious beliefs and practices. Remind them to be respectful of other people's religious beliefs and practices.

After a few minutes, have youth switch roles so that each person gets to experience sharing the Christian faith with a friend from another faith.

As they discuss in their groups of three, circulate among them and listen. When all persons have had a chance to be "the Christian" in their group, come back together as one large group. Ask youth to give examples of statements they made when telling their other faith friends about Christianity. If youth have trouble doing this assignment, use some of the following exchanges as examples:

Children of the One God: Judaism and Islam

Leader's Guide

and explain the basic beliefs of his or her faith. If your community is small and not very diverse, check at a nearby university, synagogue, or mosque (in a larger city). If you are unable to coordinate a personal visit, consider a phone conference using a speaker phone.

Provide copies of Three Related Religions on page 53, study resources, large sheets of paper, and markers.

Consider using one of the videos suggested on page 6 during the activity.

LOOK FOR LIFE

Muslim: I believe in only one God, Allah, who made everything. I pray to Allah five times each day, facing to the East.

Christian: That's great! I also believe in only one God, who I simply call God. I don't pray five times every day, but I usually pray before meals, before going to bed, and before tests.

Jew: Like the two of you, I also believe in only one God, but God's name is so holy that I don't say it often. I pray daily to God, sometimes in English, sometimes in Hebrew.

Christian: At church every Sunday, they take up an offering. I usually put in a quarter.

Muslim: My family gives two and one-half percent of everything we make to the poor.

Jew: My family tithes—gives ten percent of our income—to the Temple.

Christian: How about that; my parents tithe too! They give ten percent to the church. But I know some other families who probably don't even give one percent to the church. If they did, we could provide more for the homeless.

Muslim: Every Muslim in our community gives at least two and one-half percent to the poor; it's required.

Jew: Each year, boys aged thirteen and older are required to fast during Yom Kippur. I've fasted during Yom Kippur for the past two years to prepare for my thirteenth birthday this year.

Muslim: When is Yom Kippur?

Jew: It's in October this year. It moves around every year.

Christian: Kind of like Easter. Easter's on a different Sunday every year, but always in March or April. But we don't fast on Easter. The only time I've fasted was when my youth group did the thirty-hour famine.

Muslim: Ramadan also moves around every year. This year it's either late October or early November. It lasts for a month, and we fast from sunrise to sunset every day during Ramadan.

Christian: Wow, that's got to be tough.

Muslim: You get used to it.

QTJ: Quiet Time Journaling (6–8 minutes)

Pass out student journals. Allow youth five minutes to answer the questions on pages 18–19. Play soft, background music while they work.

Continue the Creed (4–8 minutes)

Ask youth if there is a statement based on today's topic that they would like to add to the group creed. Work together to refine the statement, then add to the chart. Read aloud the work-in-progress creed to close the session.

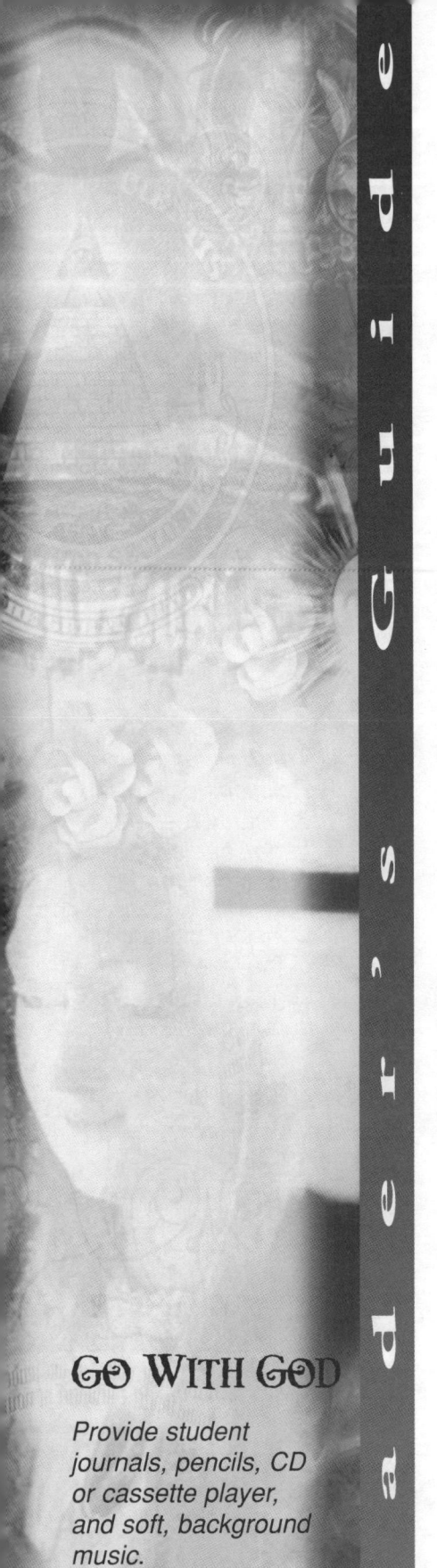

GO WITH GOD

Provide student journals, pencils, CD or cassette player, and soft, background music.

Display creed-in-progress.

Choosing Jesus: The Real Deal on the Spiritual Menu

Faith in a Hurting World: Buddhism

Topic: The Basics of Buddhism

Scripture: Lamentations 3:19-24; James 5:13; 1 Peter 4:19; Galatians 6:2; 1 Thessalonians 5:11; Romans 12:12, 15, 21

Key Verse: "The steadfast love of the LORD never ceases, [God's] mercies never come to an end; ... therefore I will hope in [God]" (Lamentations 3:22, 24b).

Take-Home Learning: God's steadfast love, especially as shown in the self-sacrificing suffering, death, and resurrection of Jesus Christ, gives Christians hope in the midst of suffering.

Younger Youth and This Topic

Members of the Millennial generation tend to be socially conscious and interested in service projects and volunteering. But the words *self-sacrifice* or *suffering* are less likely to be standards in their vocabularies. Doing good deeds helps them to feel good about themselves, to learn that their actions can make a difference, and to experience a sense of personal accomplishment. Suffering is something they—and most of us—want to avoid at all costs.

Help youth to see that the call of Christ is to selflessness and to view the world as Jesus did. Encourage youth to move beyond the idea that suffering is something God causes to the concept that suffering is something God works in the midst of. Youth should come to understand that God suffers with us. Teach youth that the faith of Buddhists enables them to deal with their suffering and that Christian faith gives us hope, which can help us in all circumstances.

Theology and This Topic

Since Christianity, Judaism, and Islam all share a common concept of God as well as some common Scriptures, Christians can often accept that each faith holds at least some truth. This acceptance becomes more difficult once you look beyond these three faiths. For example, how many Christians can accept Wicca as having a true understanding of God? And how can we reconcile Christianity with Buddhism since basically Buddhism has no "supreme being" at the center of its faith?

Faith in a Hurting World: Buddhism

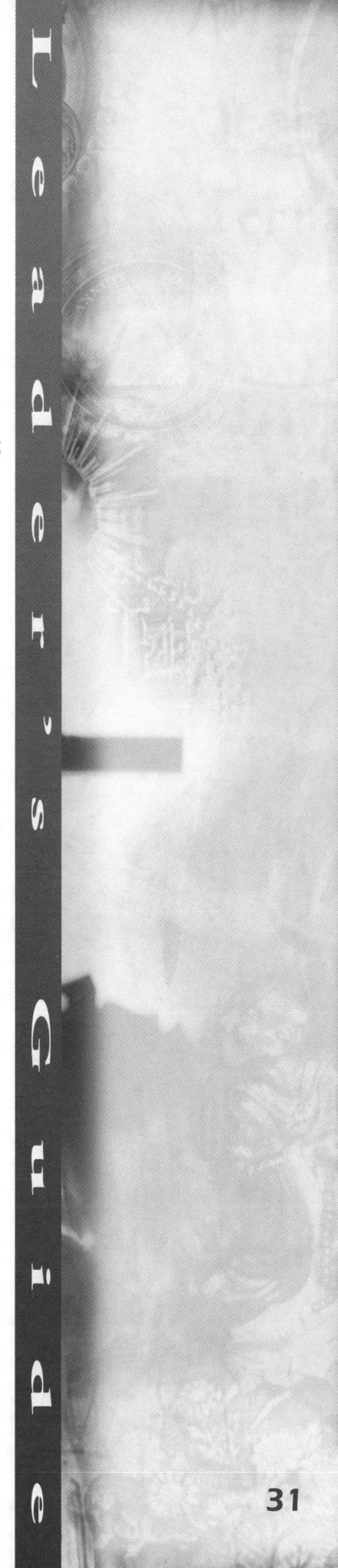

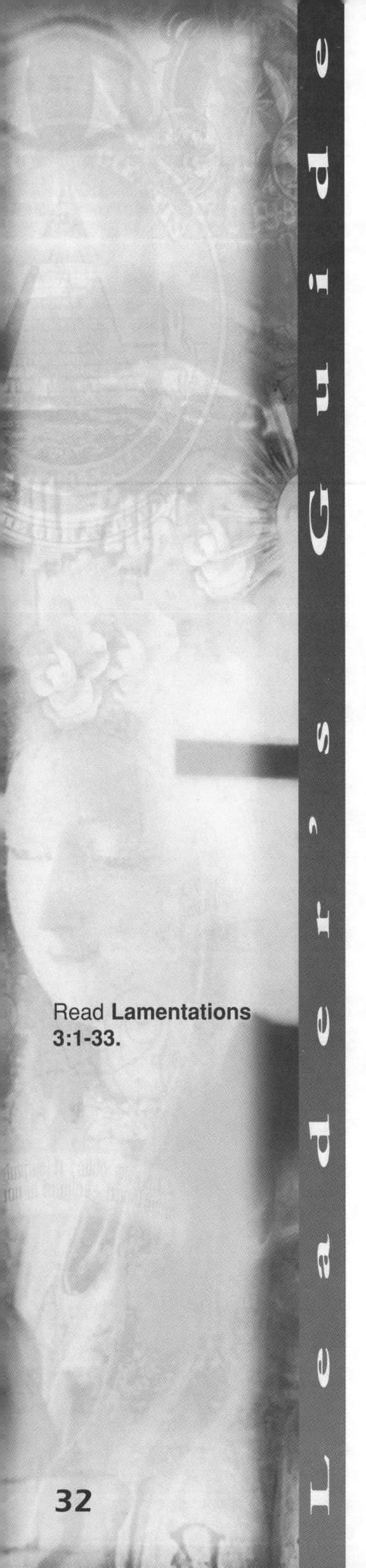

Again, we are confronted by the practical realities we discover once we become acquainted with members of other faiths. Often they are not as "misguided" as we might have once supposed; they, too, have profound beliefs and meaningful practices of faith that sustain them through life's suffering. Regardless of our faith, we share a common experience as humans; we confront suffering, pain, loss, and death in our lives, and faith is the element that empowers us to find meaning in and through those experiences.

Christians believe that sin or separation from God creates suffering for humans in a myriad of ways. Sometimes the results are direct consequences of one's own choices. Other times suffering is a result of someone else's sin, and the victim is truly innocent. Jesus' death on the cross made it possible for people to come back into right relationship with God and sin no more. Jesus suffered in order that human suffering might be taken away, lessened, or borne with peace.

Christianity also is unique in its approach to suffering because of its assertion that God suffers as well. Theologian Andrew Sung Park has powerfully explored this idea in his book, *The Wounded Heart of God*:

"God suffers not because sin is all powerful, but because God's love for humanity is too ardent to be apathetic toward suffering humanity. No power in the universe can make God vulnerable, but a victim's suffering breaks the heart of God. …To me, God suffers for the Son on the cross not only out of God's love for the Son, but also God's love for humanity. God's love for humans suffers on the cross. The cross represents God's full participation in the suffering of victims. That is, Jesus's death was the example of an innocent victim's suffering in which God was *fully* present. Yet every victim's suffering also involves God's presence."[1]

God's steadfast love, God's presence with us, and the ultimate triumph of Christ over the cross give Christians hope in the midst of suffering.

You and the Scripture

Read **Lamentations 3:1-33.**

Lamentations is not a book we often read in church; yet its cries of pain can give words to our own feelings. Which of the images in verses 1–18 captures your experience with suffering? If these descriptions do not fit, how would you describe your pain?

The statement of faith in verses 19–24 is a turning point. The speaker begins a shift from blaming God for the affliction (verse 1) to remembering the character of God (love and mercy). He draws hope from God's compassion (see verses 31–33). What experiences and knowledge of God give you hope when you suffer?

---

[1] Reprinted from *The Wounded Heart of God: The Asian Concept of Han and the Christian Doctrine of Sin,* by Andrew Sung Park. Copyright © 1993 by Abingdon Press. Used by permission.

Choosing Jesus: The Real Deal on the Spiritual Menu

Faith in a Hurting World: Buddhism

Scripture: Lamentations 3:19-24; James 5:13; 1 Peter 4:19; Galatians 6:2; 1 Thessalonians 5:11; Romans 12:12, 15, 21

Take-Home Learning: God's steadfast love, especially as shown in the self-sacrificing suffering, death, and resurrection of Jesus Christ, gives Christians hope in the midst of suffering.

🔑 indicates key activity. If time is limited, focus here.

ACTIVITY	TIME	PREPARATION	SUPPLIES
GET READY			
In the Midst of Suffering	6–8 minutes	Prepare chart with three questions. Collect newspapers and news magazines.	Large sheet of paper, markers, variety of newspapers and news magazines
JUMP IN			
Begin the Dialogue	10–16 minutes	Invite a member of the Buddhist community to visit and explain beliefs.	No supplies
OR			
🔑 Faith in Focus II	12–18 minutes	Duplicate World Religions Comparison Chart 1 on page 54.	Copies of handouts, study resources, large sheets of paper, markers
LOOK FOR LIFE			
Two Stories on Suffering	8–12 minutes	Review Bible stories suggested in the activity.	Bibles
OR			
🔑 Hope—The Antidote	10–12 minutes	Review activity on page 35.	Bibles, student journals, pencils
GO WITH GOD			
🔑 QTJ: Quiet Time Journaling	5 minutes	Display group creed in meeting room.	Bibles, student journals, CD or cassette player, background music, marker
Continue the Creed	4–5 minutes		

Faith in a Hurting World: Buddhism

33

GET READY

Provide a large sheet of paper, markers, and a variety of newspapers and news magazines.

Before the session, write the three questions in the activity "In the Midst of Suffering," on a large sheet of paper and post in the meeting room.

JUMP IN

Invite a member of the Buddhist community to visit and explain his or her basic beliefs. If your community is small or not diverse, check for possibilities in a nearby university or larger city. If you are unable to coordinate a personal visit, consider arranging a phone conference using a speaker phone.

Provide Bibles, copies of World Religions Comparison Chart 1 on page 54, various study resources, large sheets of paper, and markers.

Redistribute copies of Three Related Religions on page 53 if necessary.

34

In the Midst of Suffering (6–8 minutes)

Distribute a variety of newspapers and news magazines. As youth arrive, ask them to browse the materials for stories related to suffering and ways that individuals helped those who were hurting, hungry, and in need. For each article they find, ask them to determine answers to the following questions:

- Who is suffering or in need and why?
- What are they doing about it, or how are they responding?
- What are others doing to help those who are suffering or in need?

After a few minutes, have youth report on the stories they found along with their answers to the questions.

Say: "We live in a world where everyone suffers in some way, and many seem to suffer more than others. Today we're going to talk about how Buddhism responds to suffering in the world and how we as Christians should respond to suffering."

Begin the Dialogue (10–16 minutes)

If you were able to enlist a visiting speaker, introduce him or her at this time. Ask the individual to speak for five to seven minutes, then allow time for questions from the youth. Here are some questions you may want to ask:

- What are some of the most important beliefs of your faith?
- What hope does your faith give to persons who are suffering?
- What is your impression of Christians and Christianity?
- What, if anything, does your faith believe about Jesus?
- What can we do to increase our understanding of members of your faith?

OR

Faith in Focus II (12–18 minutes)

Give each youth copies of World Religions Comparison Chart 1 on page 54. Also provide encyclopedias, books, dictionaries of world religions, or other resources. (You may want to redistribute copies of page 53 as well.) Provide markers and large sheets of paper. Explain that they will have about seven minutes to learn as much as they can about Buddhism for a special news report during a nightly news show. Suggest they use the large sheets of paper to create visual aids for their presentations and to keep their report between two and three minutes.

Choosing Jesus: The Real Deal on the Spiritual Menu

Leader's Guide

Allow the reporter to present information in news-show style. Others can bring "news flashes" to the reporter during the show if they have points to add that the reporter is not covering.

Two Stories on Suffering (8–12 minutes)

Suffering is a reality in life. Your students may want to know why people, especially good people, suffer. Christians often turn to two Bible stories for their understandings: Adam and Eve and Job.

In teams of up to four persons, have the students piece together the story of Adam and Eve from what they collectively remember, putting events in sequence. After a few minutes, retell the story as a group with the various teams adding information. If facts and events are added incorrectly, correct the information or rearrange information in the proper order. Continue to the point at which God states the punishment, then read aloud verses 14–19 in Genesis 3. Ask:

- How do these verses contrast with life in the garden before Eve and Adam gave into temptation and sinned? *(These verses are the first indication of suffering.)*

Say: "Christians point to this story as a recognition that suffering is often the result of choices humans make. People may suffer directly because their own decisions result in consequences or indirectly because choices others make (often unknown to them) affect their lives.

"However, Christians also turn to the story of Job. He was a good man and suffered greatly through no wrongdoing—either his own or others'. At the end of the story, Job and God have a significant conversation in which God basically tells Job that humans cannot know everything—some things are beyond us. As people of faith, we know that not all suffering can be explained but that God is with us through it."

OR

Hope—The Antidote (10–12 minutes)

Say: "Although all Christians suffer at some point in their lives, suffering is not the focus of Christianity as it is with Buddhism."

Direct the youth to page 20 in the student journal. Explain to the youth that the word *lamentations* comes from *lament*, which means to mourn, to grieve, and to regret something deeply. Ask students to locate Lamentations 3:1-18 in their Bibles, take a few moments to look over the verses, and then call out some of the images and statements that show the depth of the man's suffering. (Consider sharing information in the margin note.) Then ask:

- How do you usually respond when life is going badly for you?

Faith in a Hurting World: Buddhism

LOOK FOR LIFE

Provide Bibles.

Provide Bibles and student journals.

Note: In Lamentations 3:1 the speaker attributes the suffering to God; however, later in the text, he begins to think differently because he knows the nature of God to be good.

Now ask youth to read Lamentations 3:19-24 and in their own words rewrite the verses in their journals. After a few minutes, invite them to read their paraphrases. Then ask:

- What change has taken place in the man? Why? (*Over time his experience and knowledge of God has shown him that God's love is steadfast; he can count on it.*)

- How can knowing that God is compassionate and merciful help you in the midst of suffering?

Direct the youth to page 21 and the statement about Jesus' suffering. After a minute or two, have youth remind one another of the ways Jesus suffered in his lifetime. If they forget or do not know, tell them about the time his hometown folks drove him out of town (Luke 4:16-30); about the Pharisees repeatedly trying to trap him; and about the events of Holy Week.

Ask:

- What did Jesus do that tells us he was greater than all that suffering? (*He endured the suffering without retaliating; he rose from the dead.*)

- How does Jesus' resurrection give us hope?

- What difference does it make when you suffer to have hope?

- What is life like for persons who have no sense of hope?

Say: "To be a Christian is to be a person of hope! Christian hope is not some nebulous feeling, rather it is a conviction. It is based on what we know about God, Jesus, and the Holy Spirit, which is God with us, helping us through our suffering."

QTJ: Quiet Time Journaling (5 minutes)

Pass out the student journals. Allow youth five minutes to answer the questions on pages 22–23. Play soft, background music as they work. Close with prayer or Continue the Creed.

OR

Continue the Creed (4–5 minutes)

Ask if there is a statement based on today's topic that they would like to add to the group creed. Work together to refine the statement, add it to the chart, then read the creed in unison to close your session.

GO WITH GOD

Provide Bibles, student journals, pencils, a CD or cassette player, and background music.

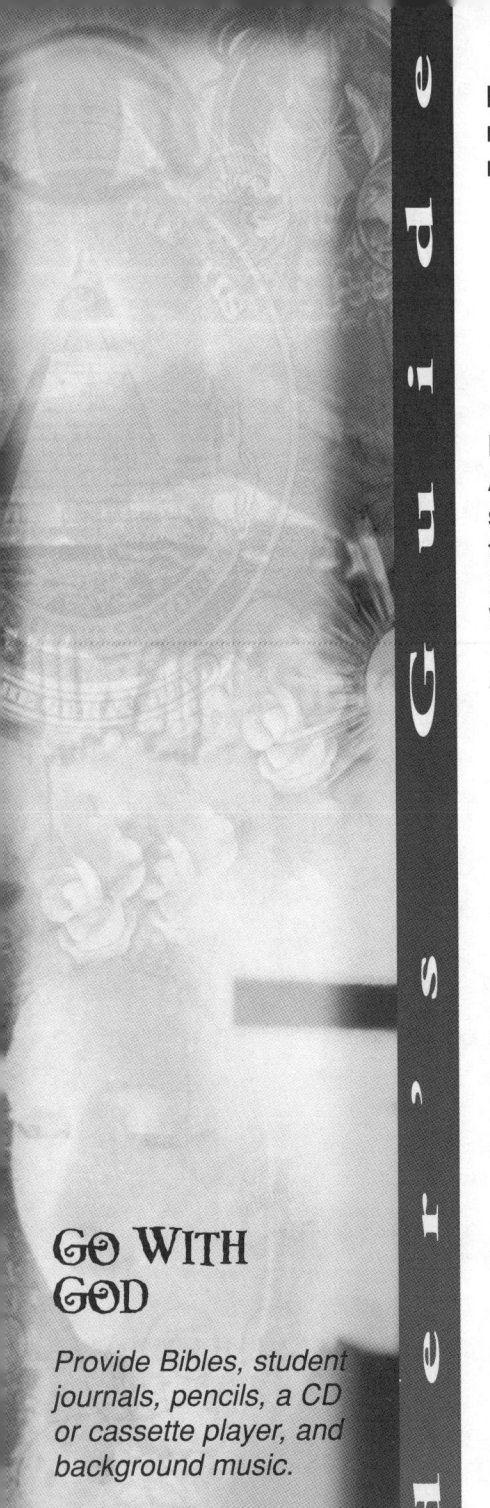

Remember to display the work-in-progress creed in the meeting room.

The hymn, "Great Is Thy Faithfulness," is based on Lamentations 3:22-23. You may wish to point that out or sing it together in the closing.

Choosing Jesus: The Real Deal on the Spiritual Menu

SESSION 6

Equal in the Sight of God: Hinduism

Topic: The Basics of Hinduism

Scripture: Exodus 20:2-6; Deuteronomy 6:4; Galatians 3:28

Key Verse: "There is no longer Jew or Greek, there is no longer slave or free, there is no longer male or female; for all of you are one in Christ Jesus" (Galatians 3:28).

Take-Home Learning: Everyone is equal when they have accepted Jesus Christ. No class, race, gender, ethnicity, or economic differences make a person greater or less in the fellowship of Jesus Christ.

Younger Youth and This Topic

Younger Youth are moving from concrete thinking to abstract thinking. The mix of youth in your group is likely to have youth from anywhere along the concrete-abstract continuum. The concepts of multiple gods and of reincarnation or transmigration of souls are more abstract than are the concepts of one God and one lifetime. Sixth through eighth graders begin to ask questions about multiple gods and multiple lifetimes, so they naturally will be intrigued by a religion that believes in these concepts.

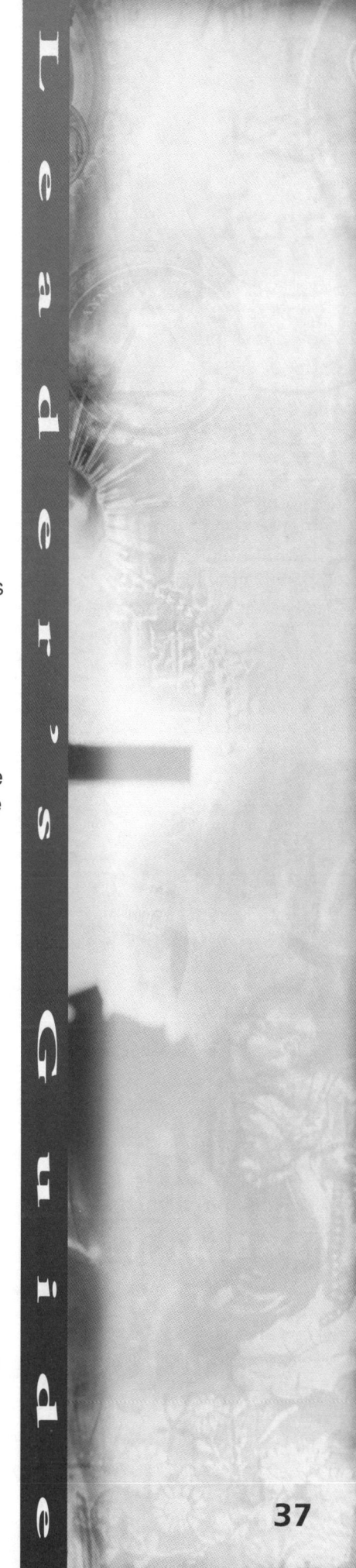

Younger youth also begin to recognize race, gender, and economic differences that may have escaped them when they were children. How they learn to relate at this age to persons who are different from them will help form these attitudes for many years—possibly a lifetime.

Theology and This Topic

Quite often churches teach youth that a "god" can be anything that they cherish too greatly, such as designer clothes, cell phones, CD players, computers, and game machines. Although this is true and important, it misses the point the biblical writers made about worshipping idols. In biblical times (both Old and New Testaments), religious people struggled with worshipping a god that they could not see. Many felt more comfortable worshipping a statue or idol that they could see, but the Jews and later the Christians considered that practice sacrilegious.

God began the Ten Commandments with "You shall have no other gods before me" and "You shall not make for yourself an idol … you shall not

Equal in the Sight of God: Hinduism

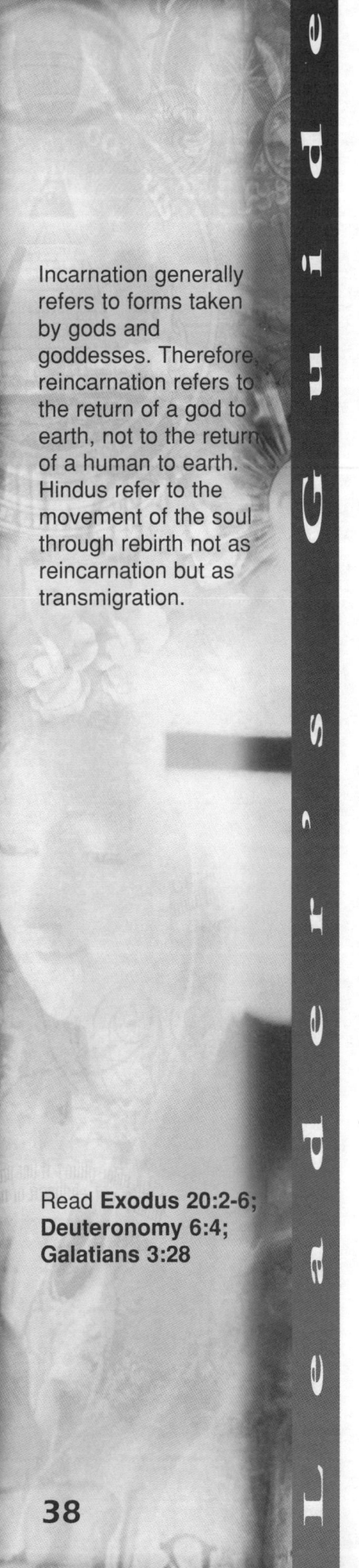

bow down to them or worship them." Throughout the Bible, idol worship is one of the worst blasphemies. Matthew 24:15 references the placing of an idol in the Temple (desolating sacrilege in the holy place), and Revelation 2:6, 14-15 condemns idol worshippers (Nicolaitans) when addressing two of the seven churches. Therefore, the aspects of many gods and of idol worship that are central to the Hindu faith are objectionable to most Christians.

Transmigration

The concept of transmigration of the soul is also unfamiliar to Christians. Hindus believe that unless a person's karma is perfect, his or her soul cannot be set free. Therefore, the soul of each person transmigrates to a new being, so that the new being can increase the positive karma. Christians believe that each person has the choice in life to accept Christ or reject Christ, and that choice leads to his or her soul achieving eternal bliss or not.

Equality

For many Christians, the most disturbing aspect of Hindu practice is the caste system. The Hindu religion has five castes or social classes. The five castes are priest (Brahmin), governing (Kshatriya), middle class (Vaisya), peasant (Sudra), and untouchable. Contact between members of different castes is strictly controlled, and untouchables have no access to the rituals of the other classes. Although the government of India has ruled the caste system to be illegal, it still exists within much of the culture. Discrimination based on caste is changing in India, especially in the larger cities, but it still exists.

A similar situation within the United States is the issue of racial equality. Christianity opposes discrimination on race (all people are equal). All United States presidents have been Christian, as well as most members of the other two branches of government. Our government has passed laws prohibiting discrimination based on race. Yet race discrimination still exists.

The main difference between these two examples is one of religious belief. Hindu belief is based on inequality; Christian belief is based on equality. In practice, people of both religions struggle.

You and the Scripture

Before teaching this session, give thoughtful consideration to each of the three major differences between Hinduism and Christianity. Do you have idols in your own life that you "worship"? Do you struggle with people not being given a second chance after death to improve their eternal situation? Do you treat all people equally, regardless of race, gender, ethnicity, economic condition, handicapping condition, and so on?

Sidebar:

Incarnation generally refers to forms taken by gods and goddesses. Therefore, reincarnation refers to the return of a god to earth, not to the return of a human to earth. Hindus refer to the movement of the soul through rebirth not as reincarnation but as transmigration.

Read **Exodus 20:2-6; Deuteronomy 6:4; Galatians 3:28**

Choosing Jesus: The Real Deal on the Spiritual Menu

Equal in the Sight of God: Hinduism

Scripture: Exodus 20:2-6; Deuteronomy 6:4; Galatians 3:28

Take-Home Learning: Everyone is equal when they have accepted Jesus Christ. No class, race, gender, ethnicity, or economic differences make a person greater or less in the fellowship of Jesus Christ.

🗝 indicates key activity. If time is limited, focus here.

ACTIVITY	TIME	PREPARATION	SUPPLIES
GET READY			
Stuck in My Head	5–7 minutes	Prepare two charts.	Several packs of sticky notes, two large sheets of paper, markers
JUMP IN			
Begin the Dialogue	10–16 minutes	Invite a member of the Hindu community to visit and explain beliefs.	No supplies
OR			
🗝 Faith in Focus III	12–18 minutes	Duplicate World Religions Comparison Chart 2 on page 55.	Copies of handouts, study resources, large sheets of paper, markers
LOOK FOR LIFE			
🗝 Choosing Jesus	15–18 minutes	Review activity on page 41.	No supplies
OR			
One God or Many; Caste About	8–12 minutes	Review Bible passages suggested in the activity.	Bibles, copies of World Religions Comparison Chart 2 (page 55)
GO WITH GOD			
🗝 QTJ: Quiet Time Journaling / Continue the Creed	5 minutes / 4–5 minutes	Display the group creed worked on during each session.	Bibles, student journals, pencils, CD or cassette player, background music

Equal in the Sight of God: Hinduism

GET READY

Provide several pads of sticky notes, markers, and two large sheets of paper.

Before the session, hang two large sheets of paper. Label one *Hinduism* and one *We're not sure*.

JUMP IN

Invite a member of the Hindu community to visit and explain the basic beliefs of his or her faith. If your community is small and not very diverse, check for possibilities at a nearby university (in a larger city). If you are unable to coordinate a personal visit, consider setting up a phone conference using a speaker phone.

Provide copies of World Religions Comparison Chart 2 (page 55), various study resources, large sheets of paper, and markers.

Redistribute copies of World Religions Comparison Chart 1 on page 54 if necessary.

Stuck in My Head (5–7 minutes)

Place a supply of sticky notes and markers on each table. As youth arrive, point out the charts and ask them to write a fact they know, a feeling or impression, or a question they'd like to have answered about Hinduism. Suggest they write using large letters so the notes can be read by others. Encourage them to be honest. When they finish writing their notes, tell them to stick them on the appropriate charts.

After everyone has arrived and you have several questions, facts, and impressions, read them to the group; ask for clarification or explanation if necessary. If you or anyone else questions the validity of a question or comment, move it to the chart labeled, *We're not sure*.

When appropriate, use the notes as a springboard for discussion. In particular, you may wish to dialogue about issues that indicate stereotypes and fears related to members of other faiths.

Begin the Dialogue (10–16 minutes)

If you've been able to enlist a visitor, introduce him or her at this time. Ask the visitor to speak for five to seven minutes and then allow time for questions from the youth. Here are some suggested questions:

- What is the name you most often use to address God and why?
- What is your impression of Christians and Christianity?
- What does your faith believe about Jesus?
- What can we do to increase understanding between the members of our two faiths?

OR

Faith in Focus III (12–18 minutes)

Give each youth copies of World Religions Comparison Chart 2 on page 55. Also provide encyclopedias, books, and dictionaries of world religions, or other resources. (You may want to redistribute copies of page 54 as well.) Provide markers and large sheets of paper. Explain that they will have about seven minutes to learn as much as they can about Hinduism for a special news report during a nightly news show. Suggest they use the large sheets of paper to create visual aids for their presentations and to keep their reports between two and three minutes. Allow the reporter to present information in a news-show style. Others can bring "news flashes" to the reporter during the show if they have points to add that the reporter is not covering.

Choosing Jesus: The Real Deal on the Spiritual Menu

🔑 Choosing Jesus (15–18 minutes)

Divide youth into groups of three. Have youth play the roles of three religious members for the group they were in (Christian, Hindu, and Buddhist). Ask them to discuss their religious beliefs and practices. Remind them to be respectful of other people's religious beliefs and practices.

After a few minutes, have youth switch roles so that each person gets to experience sharing the Christian faith with a friend from another faith.

As they discuss in their groups of three, circulate among them and listen. When all persons have had a chance to be "the Christian," come back together as one large group. Ask youth to give examples of statements they made when telling their other faith friends about Christianity.

If youth have trouble doing this assignment, direct them to the dialogue in the student journal on pages 24–25. Invite different students to read the three parts aloud as a conversation.

Ask:

- What surprised you? What was new information or a new thought?
- Have you had any conversations with persons of these faiths? What other religious beliefs or practices did you talk about?
- How do you treat persons who have different beliefs?
- Is it more important in such conversations to tell about your beliefs or to listen to the other persons'?
- How can you share God's love with persons of other religions?

OR

One God or Many; Caste About (8–12 minutes)

Divide youth into three teams and assign each one of the following Scripture passages: Exodus 20:2-6; Deuteronomy 6:4; Galatians 3:28. Point out to the students that they have discussed the Exodus and Deuteronomy passages in Session 4 about Islam and Judaism. Say, "Today we will look at just a few verses from those chapters." Ask each team to discuss the following questions and then communicate their answers with the larger group.

- How do the verses compare with the information about Hinduism found in the World Religions Comparison Chart or what you have heard in the previous part of the session?
- What does the passage say about God?
- What does the passage say about living as God's people?

Equal in the Sight of God: Hinduism

LOOK FOR LIFE

Provide Bibles and student journals.

Provide Bibles and copies of World Religions Comparison Chart 2 (page 55).

GO WITH GOD

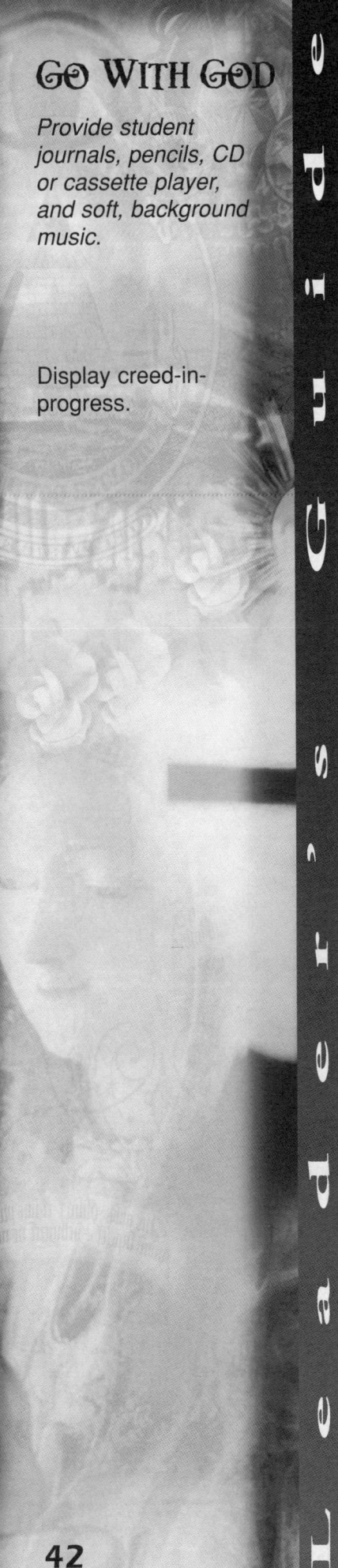

Provide student journals, pencils, CD or cassette player, and soft, background music.

Display creed-in-progress.

🗝 QTJ: Quiet Time Journaling (5 minutes)

Pass out student journals. Allow youth five minutes to read the Scriptures and answer the questions on pages 26–27. Play soft, background music while they work.
Close with prayer or Continue the Creed.

OR

Continue the Creed (4–5 minutes)

Ask youth if there is a statement based on today's topic that they would like to add to the group creed. Work together to refine the statement, then add to the chart. Read aloud the work-in-progress creed to close the session.

Choosing Jesus: The Real Deal on the Spiritual Menu

The Christ Way: Love, Kindness, and Mercy

Topic: Living As Jesus Taught Us to Live

Scripture: Luke 6:36; 10:25-37; John 13:1-17

Key Verse: "You shall love the Lord your God with all your heart, and with all your soul, and with all your strength, and with all your mind; and your neighbor as yourself" (Luke 10:27).

Take-Home Learning: The way of Jesus is an inseparable pairing of devotion to God and to neighbor.

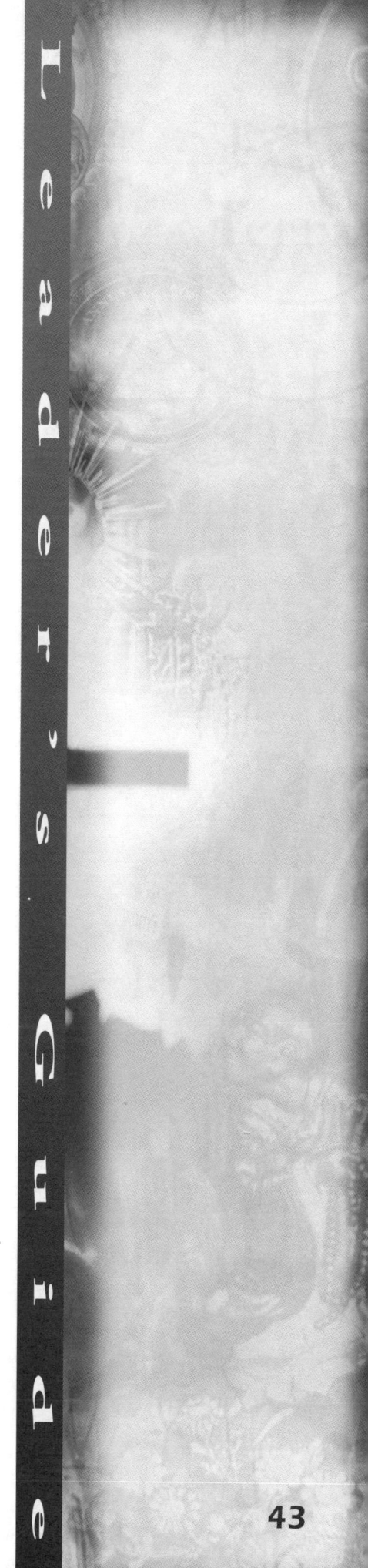

Younger Youth and This Topic

What a paradoxical time the middle school/junior high years are! On the one hand, youth are incredibly self-absorbed, seemingly far more interested in clothes, friends, and their bodies than in matters of the spirit. At the same time, surveys reveal younger youth are more interested in helping others than in anything else the church offers them. Truly this is a time in their lives when an others-focused lifestyle can be developed and encouraged.

Younger youth are experiential learners; in most cases, they learn best when they have the opportunity to do or practice something first and then reflect on what they've done. Otherwise, their lack of experience becomes a barrier to purposeful discussion. Ideally, this session would be a follow-up to a service project in which most of the youth participate.

To make the most of any service experience, prepare the youth by setting the stage and posing questions for them to think about as they begin. Then afterwards, be sure to debrief the activity and discuss the questions. Invite youth to express their feelings and insights as well. This pattern of preparing, doing, and debriefing is key in order for them to learn from their serving. This session will further enhance their understanding and commitment to love, kindness, and mercy.

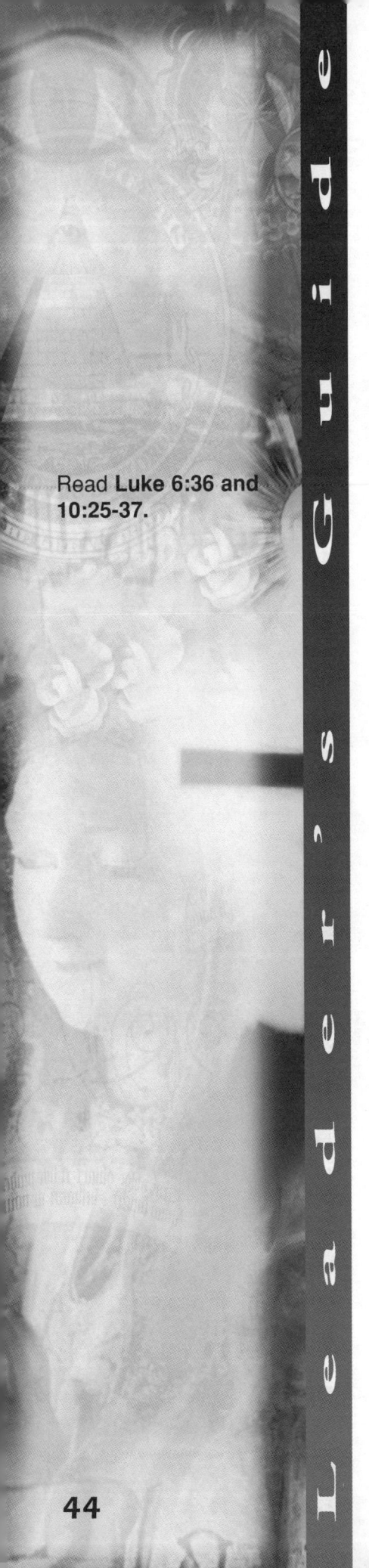

Theology and This Topic

Although religious beliefs develop in many ways, all religions attempt to give meaning to the big questions of life: Why are we here? What is our purpose? What is the meaning of suffering? Without a framework for understanding questions such as these, people often feel frustrated, alone, and lost. While many religions share common beliefs about the importance of love, justice, and service, Christianity is unique because of Christ: Our God dwelt among us and became humble as a servant. It is by following that life of selflessness that we discover meaning for our own lives.

You and the Scripture

Read **Luke 6:36 and 10:25-37.**

Which is easiest for you: loving God with your heart, soul, strength, or mind? Which is hardest for you? How do these answers shape your spirituality and practice of faith?

The phrase "love your neighbor as yourself" is probably better translated "love your neighbor in the same manner as you love yourself." In other words, the emphasis is upon caring for others as equally as you care for your own needs. What does it mean to you to love someone else in this way?

Read Luke 6:36 (from a variety of translations if possible). Various translations use words such as holy, perfect, merciful, or compassionate. But whatever the word used, the meaning gets at the deep character of God: tender mercy and compassion. What would your life look like if you showed others the compassion and mercy of God?

Choosing Jesus: The Real Deal on the Spiritual Menu

The Christ Way: Love, Kindness, and Mercy

Scripture: Luke 6:36; 10:25-37; John 13:1-17

Take-Home Learning: The way of Jesus is an inseparable pairing of devotion to God and to neighbor.

🗝 indicates key activity. If time is limited, focus here.

ACTIVITY	TIME	PREPARATION	SUPPLIES

GET READY

| Extraordinary Service Awards | 8–12 minutes | Prepare certificates for youth to complete. | Variety of paper types, pens, markers, scissors, ribbon, stickers |

JUMP IN

🗝 | Service With a Smile ... and a Towel | 12–15 minutes | Prepare the tub of water and towel strips before the session. | Small, plastic tub, several small towels, a towel cut into strips, permanent markers |

LOOK FOR LIFE

🗝 | Three Ways of Living | 7–12 minutes | Duplicate copies of The Way Of ... on page 56. | Copies of handout, pencils |

GO WITH GOD

🗝 | QTJ: Quiet Time Journaling | 5–7 minutes | Obtain a CD or cassette player and soft, background music. | Bibles, student journals, pencils, CD or cassette player, background music |

OR

| Continue the Creed | 6–8 minutes | Display the group creed. | Markers |

AND

🗝 | Three Roads | 8–12 minutes | Review activity on pages 47–48. | Student journals, pencils |

The Christ Way: Love, Kindness, and Mercy

45

GET READY

Provide a variety of paper types, pens, markers, scissors, ribbon, and stickers.

If possible, make or buy 8 1/2-by-11 stationary with a certificate-like border.

JUMP IN

Provide a small, plastic tub, several small towels, a towel cut into strips, and permanent markers.

During the week, arrange with one of the students to be the person whose feet are to be washed.

Before the session, fill the small, plastic tub with hot, soapy water. Hide the tub with the small towels in a cabinet, closet, or box along with another towel cut into small, bookmark-length strips.

Extraordinary Service Awards (8–12 minutes)

As youth arrive, ask them to design one or more awards for someone they know who has given time and love in a selfless way. (Be prepared with a list of suggestions for those who are slow to have ideas: Sunday school teachers, volunteer youth leaders, church library assistants, nursery workers, and so on.) Offer help to any who have difficulty composing the wording on the certificate. Suggest simple phrases they can use. (For example, "For compassionate and selfless service as a _____, we present you with this certificate of recognition and thanks," or "Thanks for all you do to help with_____.") When the youth have finished, decide as a group when and how you will present the awards.

Service With a Smile ... and a Towel (12–15 minutes)

Ask: "Stores and restaurants often display a motto that they encourage employees to follow: 'Service with a Smile.' What do you think this statement means?" Wait for a few comments.

Say: "Generally, we expect this type of service. We are surprised when a cashier treats us in an unkind and unfriendly manner. But sometimes people do something for us that is completely unexpected. They show us love, kindness, or mercy when we don't deserve it." Ask:

- Can you think of a time in your life when someone showed you love, kindness, or mercy in an unexpected way?

Invite a few of the youth to tell about their experiences. Be prepared to tell a story of your own if none of the youth share.

Take out the tub of water and the towels and set them at the feet of the volunteer selected prior to the session. Kneel before the person, then silently take off the shoes and socks and wash his or her feet.

When you have finished, retell or read aloud the story of Jesus washing the disciples' feet in John 13:1-17. Then ask the volunteer, "What was it like to have your feet washed?" After he or she responds, ask the group:

- What were you thinking as you watched (insert name) get his or her feet washed?

- How do you think the disciples felt when Jesus began to wash their feet?

- What was unexpected about Jesus acting in this way? (*It was not the way a teacher was expected to treat pupils; it was not an act friends did for one another; it was not what the disciples felt the Messiah should do; it was the job of a slave or servant.*)

Pass out the strips of towel and permanent markers. Ask the youth to write on the strips words or phrases that will remind them of what Jesus

Choosing Jesus: The Real Deal on the Spiritual Menu

did and asked his disciples to do. Encourage the youth to place their towel strips in frequently used books or other locations where they will see them often.

Three Ways of Living (7–12 minutes)

Divide the group into three teams. Give each team one of the assignments from The Way Of ... on page 56. Ask them to read and follow the directions for preparing a skit. Allow approximately five minutes for work. Walk around while teams are working and offer to help if necessary. When you sense that the teams are ready, call for presentations. When the teams have finished, ask:

- How did the Samaritan's actions demonstrate what the lawyer in the Bible passage said was the law—to love God with all your heart, soul, mind, and strength and to love your neighbor as yourself?

QTJ: Quiet Time Journaling (5–7 minutes)

Pass out the student journals. Allow five minutes for youth to answer questions on pages 28–29. Play soft, background music as they work.

OR

Continue the Creed (6–8 minutes)

Ask if there is a statement based on today's topic that they would like to add to the group creed begun in the first session. Work together to refine the statement, add to the chart, then read in unison to close your session.

AND

Three Roads (8–12 minutes)

Pass out the student journals and pencils. Then ask youth to turn to page 30 and spend a few minutes looking at the illustration.

Wait for a bit, then say: "The road in this illustration forks and leads into three new roads. The road on the left represents the way of evil—of living a life that is harmful to others. Along that road, I'd like you to write words or draw symbols of actions and attitudes that represent that kind of life." Wait a few minutes, then ask a few youth to explain one of the words or symbols they wrote or drew.

The Christ Way: Love, Kindness, and Mercy

LOOK FOR LIFE

Provide copies of The Way Of ... on page 56 and pencils.

GO WITH GOD

Provide Bibles, student journals, pencils, CD or cassette player, and soft, background music.

Display group creed for the final session.

Provide student journals and pencils.

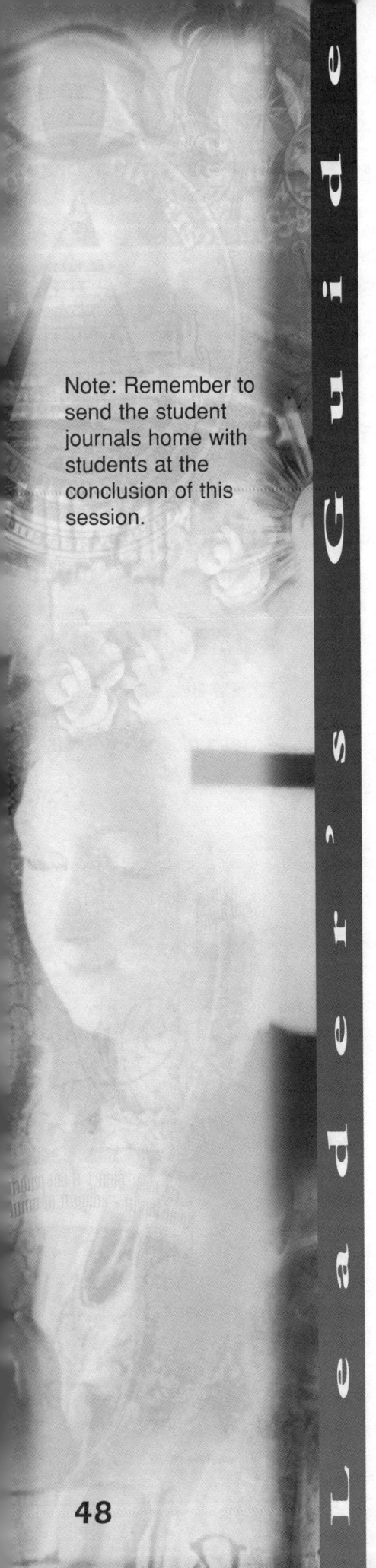

Note: Remember to send the student journals home with students at the conclusion of this session.

Say: "The road on the right represents a life lived selfishly—focusing only on personal wants and desires. Along that road, write or draw words or images that represent that kind of lifestyle." Again wait a few minutes, then ask several youth to share one of the words or images they wrote or drew.

Say: "The middle road represents the way of Jesus, a way of selfless love and compassion for others. Take a couple of minutes to write any words or draw any images that come to mind when you think of that kind of life." When everyone is finished, ask several youth to explain one of the words or images they wrote or drew.

To conclude the session, ask the group to form a circle and lay their road pictures on the floor in front of them. Ask them to imagine they are about to step on that road. Close with a prayer such as:

> "Lord, we are faced with many choices on our journey of faith. Sometimes we must decide how to respond in the face of evil. And sometimes we hurt others with our words or actions. Help us to turn from those ways of life that are harmful to us and to others.
>
> "Sometimes we live selfishly, focusing only on our own desires and forgetting about all of your people. Help us to turn away from our personal ways and toward you and all of your children.
>
> "We want to walk the road that Jesus walked—the road of servanthood and of giving our lives away for others. Be with us as we step out in faith on that road. Amen."

Choosing Jesus: The Real Deal on the Spiritual Menu

Session 1 Reproducible Page

BASIC BELIEFS QUIZ

Instructions: Which of the statements below reflect commonly held Christian beliefs? Mark each statement with an A, B, or C.

A. All Christians believe this.
B. Some Christian groups believe this.
C. Christians don't believe this.

___ 1. When you die, you will be reincarnated as a better person.

___ 2. Jesus was a great prophet, but he was not the Son of God.

___ 3. To receive eternal life, you only have to do good works and help others.

___ 4. Jesus was not a real human being; instead he was a spirit that looked like us.

___ 5. There are hundreds of commandments in the Bible, and we should follow them all.

___ 6. The only name we should call God is Father.

___ 7. When Jesus was placed in the tomb, he wasn't really dead, but instead he had passed out. That's why he came back to life.

___ 8. Only 144,000 people will go to heaven at the end of time.

___ 9. We no longer need to read the Old Testament because we have the New Testament.

___ 10. There are other Scriptures besides the Bible that we should read to understand God's will.

___ 11. Jesus knew from the beginning of his life that he would die to save others from sin.

___ 12. Satan is not a real "person" but a literary figure who represents the presence of evil in the world.

___ 13. If we have enough faith, God will heal us from our diseases and we won't need doctors.

___ 14. God's forgiveness is available to some people and not to others.

___ 15. The Holy Spirit is Jesus' presence, guiding and directing us.

___ 16. We experience God in three natures or forms: as our God, in the person of Jesus, and through the presence of the Holy Spirit.

___ 17. Our most important commandment is to love God and to love our neighbor.

___ 18. God literally created the world in six days.

___ 19. Though Jesus isn't physically alive in the world today, he is present in the church—the body of Christ.

___ 20. Only some denominations are true expressions of Christian faith; the rest are false.

___ 21. Not everything in the Bible happened exactly as it is written, but we can still call it the Word of God because in it we hear God's voice.

___ 22. You must pray before every meal and at least twice more each day.

Permission is granted to photocopy this page for use in groups studying *Choosing Jesus*.
© 2003 by Abingdon Press.

Session 2 Reproducible Page

ENCOUNTERS OF ANOTHER KIND

Scripture	What was going on?	What was the message?	What was the response?	What did he/she/they do?
Exodus 3:1-10				
Exodus 23:20-25; 24:3				
Judges 13:1, 24				
1 Kings 19:1-8				
Matthew 1:18-25				
Acts 5:17-21a				
Acts 8:25-40				

Permission is granted to photocopy this page for use in groups studying Choosing Jesus.
© 2003 by Abingdon Press.

Session 3 Reproducible Page

Three Questions

Instructions: Cut apart sections. Divide youth into teams and give one section to each. Ask teams to circle the number beside the answer or answers that represent what Christians believe is the truth based on the Scriptures listed with each question and facts already learned.

What do these Scriptures say about who Jesus was?

Matthew 16:13-17; Romans 8:3; 1 John 4:9

1. A great prophet among other equally great prophets
2. God in human form
3. A "teacher of light" who can bring us out of darkness
4. A god who is the highest among all the other gods that exist
5. A creation of God, just as we are creations of God
6. The Messiah, the Son of God, who saves us from sin
7. A leader who only partially reveals God to us
8. One of three Gods—the others being the Creator and the Holy Spirit

---

What do these Scriptures state about the authority of the Bible?

Deuteronomy 4:1-2; Psalm 119:105; 2 Timothy 3:14-17

1. A great book that we should read alongside other great spiritual books
2. A book that is complete only when new, recently discovered texts are added
3. True Scripture that has been improved upon by a new revelation
4. A collection of sixty-six different books with very little in common
5. A collection of sixty-six different books with much in common
6. Scripture that is sufficient (all we need) for our faith
7. A book with hidden truths that only special leaders such as ministers can interpret

---

What do these Scriptures teach about grace and doing good works?

Ephesians 1:7-8a; 2:8; 2 Timothy 1:8-9a; 1 Peter 4:10

1. Forgiveness for our sin comes only through the action of a priest or minister/leader.
2. Works of caring, compassion, and righteousness are responses to God's grace.
3. We must become better people to receive God's favor.
4. God will love us only if we do good works.
5. We gain our salvation if we do God's will.
6. Grace is God's free, unconditional love and acceptance of us.
7. We are saved by our works—the good things we do in life. Those same works allow us to receive the grace of Christ.
8. Our good works should be accomplished so that the church and its leaders profit.

Permission is granted to photocopy this page for use in groups studying Choosing Jesus.
© 2003 by Abingdon Press.

Session 4 Reproducible Page

WHERE IN THE WORLD ARE THEY?

Note: Only countries with a population more than ten million are listed (except Israel). Numbers indicate percentages and don't necessarily total one hundred percent due to rounding or lack of statistical data.

Afghanistan—Islam (100)
Albania—Islam (70); Christian (30)
Algeria—Islam (99)
Angola—Christian (85); Other (15)
Argentina—Christian (94); Jewish (2); Other (4)
Australia—Christian (76); Other (24)
Bangladesh—Islam (83); Hindu (16)
Belarus—Christian (99)
Belgium—Christian (75)
Bolivia—Christian (85)
Brazil—Christian (90)
Burkina Faso—Islam (50); Christian (10); Other (40)
Cambodia—Buddhist (95)
Cameroon—Other (51); Christian (33); Islam (16)
Canada—Christian (72)
Chile—Christian (99)
China—None (most); Islam (3); Christian (1)
Columbia—Christian (95)
Congo—Christian (70); Islam (10); Other (20)
Cuba—Christian (85)
Czech Republic—Christian (48); None (40)
Ecuador—Christian (95)
Egypt—Islam (94); Christian (6)
Ethiopia—Christian (35); Islam (40); Other (25)
France—Christian (83); Islam (7); Judaism (1)
Germany—Christian (72); Islam (2); Other/None (26)
Ghana—Islam (30); Christian (24); Other (38)
Greece—Christian (98); Islam (1)
Guatemala—Christian (most)
Hungary—Christian (93); Other/None (7)
India—Hindu (83); Islam (11); Christian (4)
Indonesia—Islam (87); Christian (9); Hindu (2)
Iran—Islam (99)
Iraq—Islam (97); Christian/Other (3)
Israel—Judaism (82); Islam (14); Christian (2)
Italy—Christian (98)
Ivory Coast—Other (60); Islam (23); Christianity (17)

Japan—Buddhist (most); Christian (1)
Kazakhstan—Islam (47); Christian (46); Other (7)
Kenya—Christian (76); Islam (16); Other (8)
Madagascar—Other (52); Christian (41); Islam (7)
Malawi—Christian (75); Islam (20)
Mali—Islam (90); Other (9); Christian (1)
Mexico—Christian (100)
Morocco—Islam (99); Christian (1)
Mozambique—Other (60); Christian (30); Islam (10)
Myanmar—Buddhist (90); Christian (5); Islam (4)
Nepal—Hindu (90); Buddhist (5); Islam (3)
Netherlands—Christian (59); Islam (3)
Nigeria—Islam (50); Christian (40); Other (10)
North Korea—Buddhism and Other (most)
Pakistan—Islam (97)
Peru—Christian (100)
Philippines—Christian (94); Islam (5)
Poland—Christian (100)
Portugal—Christian (98); Other (2)
Romania—Christian (82)
Russia—Christian (most); Islam
Saudi Arabia—Islam (100)
Senegal—Islam (92); Other (6); Christian (2)
South Africa—Christian (68); Islam (2); Hindu (2); Other (28)
South Korea—Christian (48); Buddhist (49)
Spain—Catholic (99)
Sri Lanka—Buddhist (69); Hindu (15); Islam (8); Christian (8)
Sudan—Islam (70); Other (20); Christian (5)
Syria—Islam (90); Christian (10)
Taiwan—Islam (22); Other (15); Christian (3)*
Tanzania—Christian (40); Islam (33)
Thailand—Buddhist (94); Islam (4); Hindu (1)
Uganda—Christian (66); Islam (16)
Ukraine—Christian (93); Judaism (2)
United States—Christian (86); Judaism (2); None (7); Other (5)
Uzbekistan—Islam (88); Christian (9); Other (3)
Venezuela—Christian (98)
Vietnam—Buddhist, Christian, Islam, Other
Yemen—Islam (100)
Yugoslavia—Christian (70); Islam (20); Other (10)
Zimbabwe—Christian (25); Other (75)

Permission is granted to photocopy this page for use in groups studying *Choosing Jesus*.
© 2003 by Abingdon Press.

Session 4 Reproducible Page
Three Related Religions

Judaism (twelfth-largest religion)

Judaism began over four thousand years ago with a people called the Hebrews. During an age in which other religions taught that there were many gods, Judaism's most important teaching was that there is just one God. This belief is known as "monotheism."

Over time, a collection of books, known as the Hebrew Scriptures, developed. It describes the covenant that God the Creator made with the Hebrew people. It teaches that all of humanity is created in the image of God and thus should be treated with dignity and respect. The Scriptures are clear that God expects people to worship no other gods and to do what is merciful and just in God's eyes.

Jews see history as the story of God's plan for all of humanity. Through the Jews, God's "chosen people," God is leading humanity toward a purpose that God desires. Jews also believe that God's laws must come first in the lives of believers.

Christianity (largest religion)

Originally a sect of Judaism, Christianity developed In Israel between 30–100 A.D. and quickly spread throughout the Roman Empire and eventually the world. At the center of Christianity is the person Jesus, a Jew who spent about three years preaching, teaching, and healing while he traveled the country with twelve disciples. His teachings inflamed some Jewish leaders, and he was eventually executed by crucifixion. His followers believe that after three days he was raised from the dead and is the Son of God, fully human and fully divine. Because Jesus is fully human, he experienced and understands human suffering; and because he is fully divine, his resurrection shows triumph over sin, which causes suffering, and gives humans hope in the midst of pain.

Christianity spread because its followers believe they are instructed by Jesus to make disciples of all people and all nations. Christianity is unique because of its doctrine of the Trinity, or one God present in three "persons": God, the Creator of the universe; Jesus, in whom God took on human form; and the Holy Spirit, the spiritual presence of God that guides and works in persons today. In addition to the Hebrew Scriptures (Old Testament), Christians follow a second collection of twenty-seven books known as the New Testament. Christians are those who believe and accept Jesus as the Messiah and as their Savior from sin and who follow his teachings.

Islam (second-largest and fastest-growing religion)

The word *Islam* means "submission" or "surrender," and a Muslim or person who practices Islam is one who submits. In every part of their lives, Muslims seek to submit to the will of the one true God, Allah—the same God of the Jews and Christians. Islam was founded during the early seventh century A.D. by the prophet Muhammad who felt he was called by God to warn and instruct people to worship only God. Muslims revere the prophets Adam, Noah, Moses, Jesus, and many others, but Muhammad is believed to be God's final prophet. Their sacred book is called the Koran (Qur'an), which Muslims consider to be Allah's final book, transmitted through the angel Gabriel directly to Muhammad.

Five Pillars of Islam define the practice of Muslims. First, a Muslim must confess and affirm the statement, "There is no God but Allah, and Muhammad is the Prophet of Allah." Second, Muslims pray five times each day at designated times and in certain prescribed ways. Third, Muslims must give at least two-and-one-half percent of their wealth to the poor. Fourth, Muslims must fast from sunrise to sunset during the month of Ramadan. Finally, Muslims must—if at all possible—make a pilgrimage to the holy city of Mecca at least once during their lives.

Permission is granted to photocopy this page for use in groups studying *Choosing Jesus*.
© 2003 by Abingdon Press.

Session 5 Reproducible Page

WORLD RELIGIONS COMPARISON CHART 1

	CHRISTIANITY	JUDAISM	ISLAM
View of God (Supreme Being)	Monotheistic—believe in one God who created and is creating; who governs the cosmos; all other gods are false; usually referred to as God (although other names are used).	Monotheistic—believe in one God who created and is creating; who governs the cosmos; all other gods are false; for many Jews, the name of God (*Yahweh*) is too holy to write or say, so they refer to God as Adoni or Lord.	Monotheistic—believe in one God who created and is creating; who governs the cosmos; all other Gods are false; referred to as Allah.
Founders	Jesus of Nazareth, whom believers considered the Christ (Messiah); for whom the religion is named.	Abraham is considered to be the father of the Jewish people, but Jacob (Israel), Moses, and King David figure prominently in the development of the Jewish nation.	Islam accepts many prophets, including Moses (Judaism) and Jesus (Christianity), but believes that Muhammad is the last and greatest prophet.
How People Join the Religion	Christians profess belief in Jesus Christ as Savior and are baptized.	Judaism is as much a people as a religion; most Jews are born into a Jewish family.	One becomes a Muslim by saying and believing the Shahada, "There is no god but Allah and Muhammad is the Messenger of Allah."
Sacred Writings	The Bible, containing the Old Testament (Hebrew Scriptures) and the New Testament.	Holy Scriptures, sometimes called Tanakh or Torah (what Christians refer to as the Old Testament). Later writings include the Talmud.	Qur'an (Koran), which was dictated to Muhammad by the angel Gabriel.
View of Creation/History	God created the world out of nothing and continues to govern the creation; God pronounced the creation good.	God created the world out of nothing and continues to govern the creation; God pronounced the creation good.	God created the world out of nothing and continues to govern the creation; God pronounced the creation good.
Unique or Important Beliefs	1. God is manifested in three "persons" or the Trinity: the Father/Creator; the Son (Jesus Christ); and the Holy Spirit. 2. Humans cannot atone for sins without God's grace, but God offers grace and allows humans to return to right relationship with God	1. Prayer is directed to the one and only god, with whom each person has a personal and direct relationship. 2. People have free will and there is no original sin.	Beliefs: 1. absolute oneness of Allah; 2. acceptance of Allah's prophets; 3. angels as Allah's messengers; 4. acceptance of all books that Allah has revealed; 5. resurrection and judgment at the last day; 6. predestination. Five Pillars: 1. saying the Shahada; 2. praying five times a day facing Mecca; 3. giving two and one-half percent of income to help those in need; 4. fasting during Ramadan; 5. making a pilgrimage to Mecca during one's lifetime.
Belief in Existence After Death	Each individual has only one life. Those who accept Jesus as Savior will enter Paradise and have eternal life.	Each individual has only one life. Orthodox and Conservative Jews believe that upon the coming of the Messiah, Jews who have died will be resurrected. Reconstructionist Jews believe that at death the soul rejoins the universe. Reformed Jews believe true immortality resides in memories treasured in this world by those who knew and love the deceased.	Each individual has only one life. On the Day of Judgment, God will raise all to life and judgment. Those who have lived according to the will of God will enter Paradise.
View of Jesus	Jesus was the Jewish Messiah (Christ), the fulfillment of Jewish hopes for a Redeemer. He is the Savior who died and rose to life to show his followers the way to eternal life.	Jesus was an itinerant Jewish rabbi who was executed by the Roman government.	One of many prophets; Jesus' teachings are considered important, but Allah's final revelation was given to Muhammad, not Jesus.

Session 6 Reproducible Page

WORLD RELIGIONS COMPARISON CHART 2

	CHRISTIANITY	HINDUISM	BUDDHISM
View of God (Supreme Being)	Monotheistic—believe in one God who created and is creating; who governs the cosmos; all other gods are false; usually referred to as God (although other names are used).	Polytheistic—The most popular Hindu gods are Brahma (creator), Vishnu (sustainer), and Shiva (destroyer). Hindus believe all gods they worship are expressions of one true reality (Brahman), who is beyond name and form.	Buddhists do not believe in an almighty creator god. They believe a person's future is determined by his or her actions, not by the grace or wrath of a God.
Founders	Jesus of Nazareth, whom believers considered the Christ (Messiah); for whom the religion is named.	The world's oldest religion; it has no record of a founder.	Siddhartha Gautama renounced his privileged life and experienced the suffering of the world. At the age of 35, he became enlightened (Buddha).
How People Join the Religion	Christians profess belief in Jesus Christ as Savior and are baptized.	Hinduism and India's culture are so intertwined that differentiating between them is difficult. Hindus are basically born into the religion and the caste system.	Persons do not join an organization, but simply strive to live by the Noble Eightfold Path and conform to the discipline of the Noble Truths.
Sacred Writings	The Bible, containing the Old Testament (Hebrew Scriptures) and the New Testament.	The Vedas and the Upanishads. Two epics are also considered sacred, Mahabharata and Ramayana. Within the Mahabharata is the most influential book: Bhagavad Gita.	The three branches of Buddhism (Theravada, Mahayana, and Vajrayana) each has its own sacred writings, but all three accept the Theravada as sacred.
View of Creation/ History	God created the world out of nothing and continues to govern the creation; God pronounced the creation good.	Creation is cyclical. One universe is destroyed, Brahma creates a new one; Vishnu sustains the universe for a time; then Shiva destroys it and the cycle begins again.	Creation is cyclical, having no start and no end. Life is suffering until, through adhering to the Eightfold Path, Buddhists reach the state of Nirvana.
Unique or Important Beliefs	1. God is manifested in three "persons" or the Trinity: the Father/Creator; the Son (Jesus Christ); and the Holy Sprit. 2. Humans cannot atone for sins without God's grace, but God offers grace and allows humans to return to right relationship with God.	1). The essence of each being (Atman or individual soul) is the same as the essence of the universe (Brahman or world soul). 2) There are five castes or classes in Hindu society. The caste system defines the way people relate to one another. 3) Sacrifices are made to idols of the various gods worshiped by individuals.	The Eightfold Path: 1) Right understanding; 2) Right thought; 3) Right speech; 4) Right action; 5) Right livelihood; 6) Right effort; 7) Right meditation 8) Right concentration. A summary of the Eightfold Path is: avoid evil, do good, purify your mind.
Belief About Suffering	Jesus suffered so that human suffering might be taken away, lessened, or borne with peace.	Suffering is a normal part of life, especially at the lower stages (castes); persons must perform good works to hope for a higher stage (and less suffering) in the next transmigration.	The Noble Truths: 1) Life is full of suffering. 2) People suffer because they want something that life can't give. 3) Giving up desires and attachment to this world can end suffering and bring about a state of bliss called Nirvana.
Belief in Existence After Death	Each individual has only one life. Those who accept Jesus as Savior will enter Paradise and have eternal life.	Each person's actions in life affect his or her karma. At death, the soul is transmigrated (reborn) to a higher or lower physical form. When a person's karma is perfect (all good works and no evil), a Hindu attains moksha (freedom) and leaves the wheel of life (this cycle of rebirth).	At death, life is transmigrated (reborn) to another form. When a person's desires and attachments to this world are completely given up (by walking the Eightfold Path), a person can reach a state of Nirvana.
View of Jesus	Jesus was the Jewish Messiah (Christ), the fulfillment of Jewish hopes for a Redeemer. He is the Savior who died and rose to life to show his followers the way to eternal life.	If they consider Jesus at all, it would be as a prophet who could provide enlightened teachings.	If they consider Jesus at all, it would be as a prophet who could provide enlightened teachings.

Session 7 Reproducible Page

The Way Of ...

Group 1: The Way of the Priest
Read Luke 10:25-37. Assign one person to read the following to the group:

Priests were the highest religious leaders among the Jews. They were wealthy, powerful, and enjoyed a high status that they refused to share with others. One reason the priest may have passed by without helping is that the law said that if he touched a dead body, he would be unclean. He chose to follow the law rather than act with compassion.

- What was the priest focused on the most?
- Did the priest do what the people in Jesus' audience would have expected him to do?
- What is an example of a similar behavior or way of life today?

Create a short skit representing a modern-day person who lives life in this way. Be prepared to present your skit for the large group.

Group 2: The Way of the Levite
Read Luke 10:25-37. Assign one person to read the following to the group:

Levites were the appointed helpers to priests. They dedicated themselves to serve God. Mostly, they took care of the lowly tasks in the Temple. However, Levites had little power and are listed in the Bible along with foreigners, widows, and orphans—the poorest people in the land. Helping the injured person might require money, so it would be easy for them to pass by and leave the helping to someone else.

- What was the Levite focused on the most?
- Did the Levite do what the people in Jesus' audience would have expected him to do?
- What is an example of a similar behavior or way of life today?

Create a short skit representing a modern-day person who lives life in this way. Be prepared to present your skit for the large group.

Group 3: The Way of the Samaritan
Read Luke 10:25-37. Assign one person to read the following to the group:

Samaritans were a group of people who were hated by the Jews for several reasons, but especially because they had intermarried with non-Jews many years before the time of Jesus. Jews would literally walk miles out of their way to avoid Samaria if they could. The last person a Jew would consider as an example of a good person would have been a Samaritan. The Samaritan did quite a lot to help this Jew, even spending two whole days' wages for his care.

- What was the Samaritan focused on the most?
- Did the Samaritan do what the people in Jesus' audience would have expected him to do?
- What is an example of a similar behavior or way of life today?

Create a short skit representing a modern-day person who lives life in this way. Be prepared to present your skit for the whole group.

Permission is granted to photocopy this page for use in groups studying Choosing Jesus.
© 2003 by Abingdon Press.

Retreat: All God's Children—Honoring Our Neighbor's Faith

Purpose: Through Bible studies, activities, and a discussion of the movie *Gandhi*, youth will learn about the major religions of the world and how our own faith must lead us toward peace.

Supplies: Bibles, student journals, copies of handouts, construction paper, newsprint, markers, scissors; a copy of the movie *Gandhi* (use the DVD version if available and if you have access to a DVD player); the *Reel to Real* session on *Gandhi* (www.ileadyouth.com); jewelry beads from a craft store, string, snacks, items needed for worship service.

Preparation: Review the session plans in *Reel to Real* on Gandhi, or research Gandhi's life and the history of India around the turn of the century. A helpful study guide to the movie can be found at http://www.curriculumunits.com/galileo/trials/Ghandi/framemovieguide.htm. If possible, secure informational videos on the major religions of the world such as those suggested on page 6 of this leader's guide.

Saturday

Where Do You Stand?

Play **Where Do You Stand? from Session One** (page 10).

Basic Beliefs Quiz

Conduct the **Basic Beliefs Quiz from Session One** (pages 10–11) using a game show format.

A Life in a Comma

Pass out the student journals. Ask youth to turn to "A Life in a Comma" on page 4 and answer the questions.

WWW.Ask-a-Guru.com

Pass out index cards and conduct **www.ask-a-guru.com from Session Three** (page 22).

Sample Schedule

Saturday

9:30	Arrive Unpack
10:00	Where Do You Stand?
	Basic Beliefs Quiz
	A Life in a Comma
10:30	www.ask-a-guru

A Retreat: All God's Children—Honoring Our Neighbor's Faith

Leader's Guide

	Distorting the Truth
	Three Questions
11:15	Group Games
12:00	Lunch
1:15	Learning About Our Neighbor's Faith
2:30	Free Time
3:00	Choosing Jesus
	Agreed on a Creed
4:00	Light Snack / Group Game
4:30	Field Trip
5:30	Jewish Shabbat Service

Distorting the Truth

Have youth create their own distorted drawings according to the ideas in **Distorting the Truth from Session Three** (page 23).

Three Questions

Use the Three Questions handout on page 51 to complete the **Three Questions activity from Session Three** (page 23).

Lunch

If possible, consider eating at an ethnic restaurant (such as a Jewish deli) or prepare a simple Kosher meal.

Learning About Our Neighbor's Faith

Take the youth to a local library. Divide the group into five teams and assign each team one of the major religions: Christianity, Islam, Judaism, Hinduism, and Buddhism. Distribute copies of Three Related Religions and World Religions Comparison Charts on pages 53, 54, and 55. Explain that each team will make a presentation based on the information learned. Allow thirty minutes for teams to research, then return to the retreat location to continue working on the presentations. Provide construction paper, newsprint, markers, scissors, and so on for them to create symbols, charts, or other displays for their presentations. Refer to **Faith in Focus activities from Sessions Four, Five, and Six** (pages 29, 34, and 40) for further instructions.

Choosing Jesus

Follow the instructions for **Choosing Jesus from Session Four** (page 29) and **Session Six** (page 41).

Agreed on a Creed

Review **Agreed on a Creed from Session One** (page 11), then read and talk about the creed together. Ask youth to find a quiet spot and compose a personal creed. Reassemble after fifteen minutes and allow those willing to read aloud their creeds.

Field Trip

Depart for a visit to a Jewish synagogue (see "Worship Service: A Jewish Worship Experience" on pages 63–64).

Alternate activity: If there is no Jewish synagogue in your area, visit an interfaith gathering (Hindu, Muslim, or Bahai group) if possible.

Choosing Jesus: The Real Deal on the Spiritual Menu

Dinner

After returning to the retreat location, debrief the Jewish Shabbat service while eating dinner.

Movie Time

Watch a portion of *Gandhi.* Because salt plays an important role at one point of the movie, serve salty snacks. Pass out pieces of paper and ask youth to list significant phrases or events in the movie they don't understand.

Note: If you are using the *Reel to Real Guide*, you will be able to use portions of the film effectively and shorten the time.

Movie Intermission

Take a brief break, then talk about youths' reactions to and questions from the movie thus far. Use the World Religions Comparison Charts (pages 54–55) to help clarify questions of religious beliefs and practices.

Movie Time, Part 2

Watch the next portion of *Gandhi* and discuss reactions and questions.

Devotion

You may want to focus on peace among persons of different religions, using the *Gandhi* movie as a spring board. An alternative is to talk about God's reaching out to us in diverse ways and inviting us into a holy relationship. Point out God's great love for us and how it continues to seek us. Encourage youth to respond to that love. Below are prayers and Scripture from the three major monotheistic religions. You may want to use these to create a closing prayer.

Jewish Prayer (based on Deuteronomy 6:4-9)

Hear, O Israel, the Lord is our God, the Lord is One.

Blessed be the Name of [God's] glorious kingdom for ever and ever.

And you shall love the Lord your God with all your heart and with all your soul, and with all your might. And these words that I command you today shall be in your heart. And you shall teach them diligently to your children, and you shall speak of them when you sit at home, and when you walk along the way, when you lie down and when you rise up. And you shall bind them as a sign on your hand, and they shall be for frontlets between your eyes. And you shall write them on the doorposts of your house and on your gates.

A Retreat: All God's Children—Honoring Our Neighbor's Faith

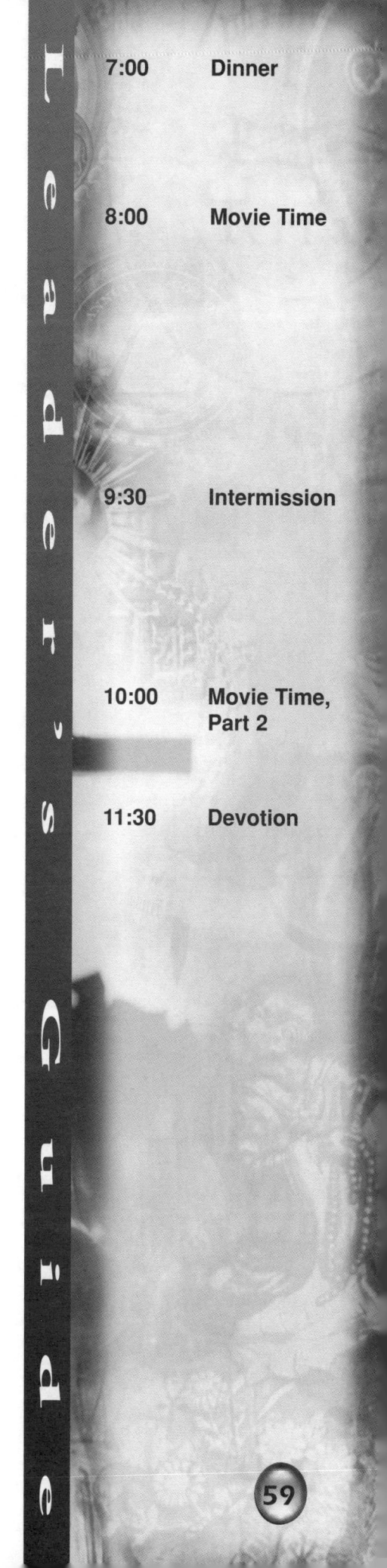

7:00	Dinner
8:00	Movie Time
9:30	Intermission
10:00	Movie Time, Part 2
11:30	Devotion

Sunday

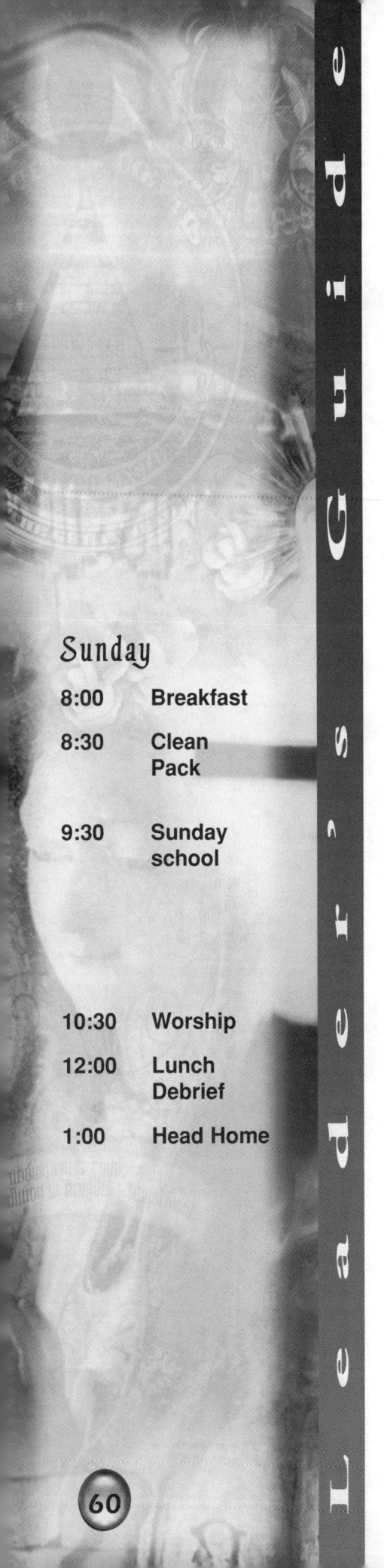

8:00	Breakfast
8:30	Clean Pack
9:30	Sunday school
10:30	Worship
12:00	Lunch Debrief
1:00	Head Home

A Christian Prayer

Loving God, giver of life and love, we thank you for all your good gifts—most especially the gift of your Son Jesus Christ, who has shown us by his life how to live and who, by his death and resurrection, makes that abundant life possible. Help us to fall more deeply in love with you so that others will see your love radiating from us. We give honor and praise to you! Amen.

Muslim: Al-Fatihah (The Opening to the Qur'an)

In the Name of God, Most Gracious, Most Merciful.

Praise be to God, the Cherisher and Sustainer of the worlds;

Most Gracious, Most Merciful.

Maker of the Day of Judgment,

Thee do we worship, and Thine aid we seek.

Show us the straight way,

The way of those on whom Thou hast bestowed Thy Grace,

those whose (portion) is not wrath,

and who go not astray. Amen.

Sunday

Sunday School

Use **Session Seven: The Christ Way: Love, Kindness, and Mercy** on page 43 to conduct the Sunday school time. Invite the youth to talk about the differences they see in the various religious traditions. Focus on the invitation of Christ to follow him in this way!

Worship

Attend worship at a church other than your own, or use "Worship: A Jewish Worship Experience" on pages 63–64. Have lunch at a nearby restaurant and talk about the worship experience.

Choosing Jesus: The Real Deal on the Spiritual Menu

Out and About: Our Neighbor Down the Street

Today's youth often visit one another's youth groups—especially for special events like lock-ins or ski trips. But they probably know very little about why the "church down the street" practices different traditions or holds different beliefs than the one they attend. Often they have practical questions about the differences between denominations, such as:

- Why do Baptist kids say we shouldn't see R-rated movies?
- Why do the Church of Christ kids say we're going to hell?
- Why do Presbyterians say my days are numbered and our lives are predestined?
- Why are laypeople in the Disciples of Christ church allowed to administer sacraments when only clergy are allowed in The United Methodist Church?
- Why does E-Free have a two-hundred member youth group when we have twenty-five?
- Why don't Catholics and many other churches allow women to serve as clergy?

One way to begin answering some of these questions is to develop a relationship with other church youth groups. For this "Out and About" session, choose another congregation's worship service to visit, and if possible, also visit a Sunday school class. Choose a denomination that is fairly different from your own congregation in theology and style. Also try to attend a service that meets about the same time as your own so that more of your youth can participate. Hopefully this visit will be the beginning of your efforts to build bridges with other congregations in your community. Millennials have a tremendous sense of togetherness and team spirit, so emphasizing our unity in Christ will connect with this generation.

The visit should not be presented as an attempt to spy on or bash another church. Approach the visit with grace and respect for the traditions of your brothers and sisters in Christ.

Follow this simple, step-by-step process:

1. Choose and contact the congregation you wish to visit. Be sure your visit doesn't interfere with a special event on their church calendar.

2. If possible, arrange for your group to meet with a pastor, Christian education director, or layleader of the congregation. Check to see if youth may ask questions about the service and differing beliefs.

3. Plan adequate time to travel to the service, attend the service, return to your church, and then debrief the experience.

4. Recruit your drivers at least three weeks in advance.

Out and About: Our Neighbor Down the Street

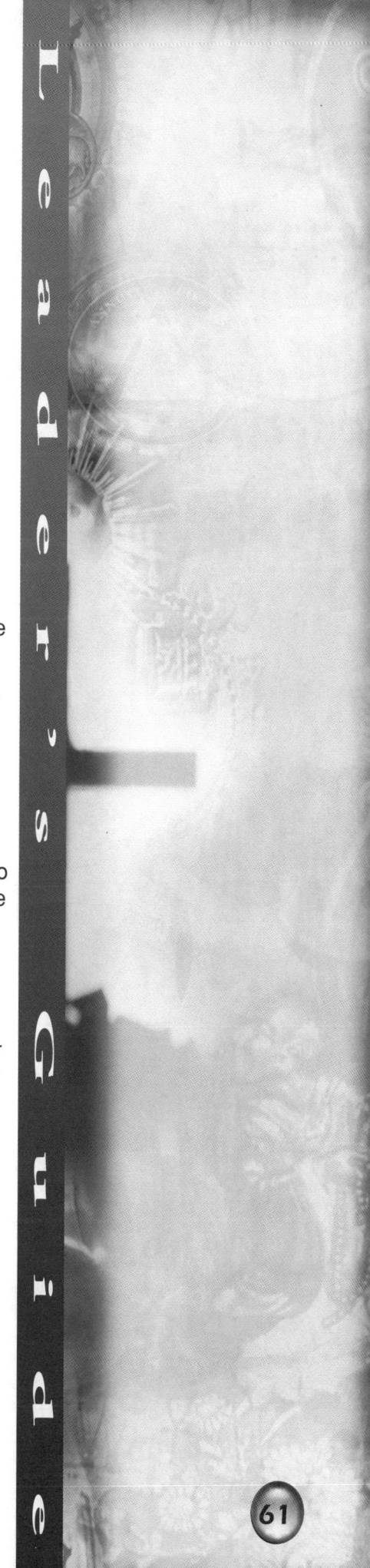

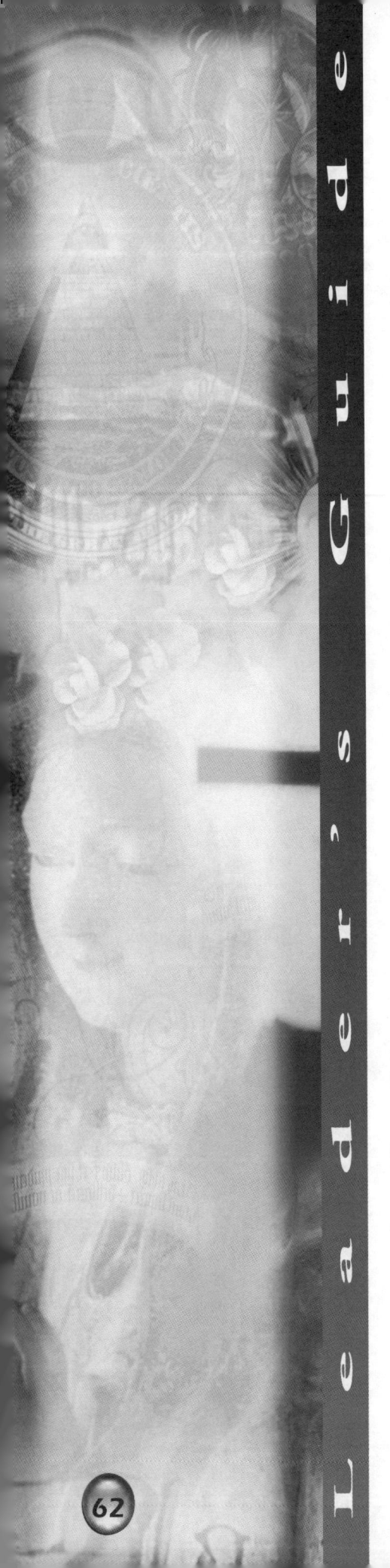

5. At least two weeks prior to the trip, send home permission forms including details regarding time, nature, and purpose of trip. If the church you are visiting has a substantially different dress code for services, inform families of this as well. Contact any youth who have been absent prior to the trip.

6. Before leaving, explain any special instructions to the youth and remind them to be polite. If you know that Communion will be served, discuss whether or not they will participate.

7. Arrive ten to fifteen minutes early so that you'll have adequate time to be seated as a group.

8. Prior to the trip, cut apart and duplicate copies of the Things to Notice handout (see below). Distribute handouts and pencils if necessary.

9. After you return to your church, spend fifteen to twenty minutes debriefing the experience by having volunteers give their answers to the questions on the handout.

10. Close with the following prayer:

> "God of many names and expressions, we are grateful for the opportunity to worship with our brothers and sisters in Christ at (insert name of church). We know that you are at work in that congregation and that the people there love and serve you too. Forgive us for the things we do to hinder unity among Christians and help us to make opportunities for dialogue with one another. Guide and direct both of our congregations as we continue our search for your truth. Amen."

--✂

Things to Notice During the Service

1. What names do they use for God? What version of the Bible do they use?

2. Which do they most emphasize: God, Jesus, or the Holy Spirit?

3. How would you describe their use of Scripture?

4. Who is allowed to preach? lead music? help with the service in other ways?

5. Which service elements are most like ours? most different?

6. How did the service make you feel? What touched you the most? What made it hard for you to worship?

Choosing Jesus: The Real Deal on the Spiritual Menu

Worship Service: A Jewish Worship Experience

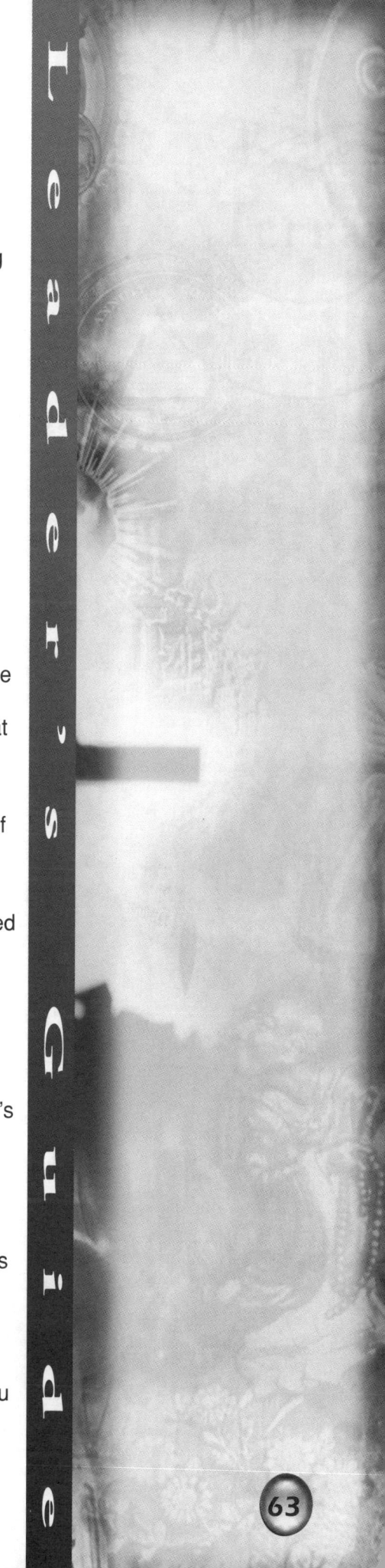

Most of your youth probably have never visited a Jewish synagogue or experienced any sort of Jewish ceremony. Here are two ideas for helping them learn more about Jewish culture and customs. The first option requires locating a Jewish synagogue in your area and attending a Saturday service. The second option requires a bit more time and effort.

Option 1: Visit a Jewish Synagogue

Check your local-area phone book or the Internet for listings of Jewish synagogues, temples, or congregations. A Reformed or Conservative Jewish congregation may be more receptive to a visit than an Orthodox congregation. Contact the congregation to learn service times and if visitors are allowed. Explain that you are interested in bringing a church youth group to experience their service and to learn more about Jewish beliefs and culture.

If possible, arrange to have someone from the congregation meet with the group before or after the service to answer any questions and provide important information. Make a point to request that they explain about Bat Mitzvah/Bar Mitzvah services. (If you can visit during one of these services, that would be even better!)

When making arrangements, remember to ask about appropriate dress, if males and females may sit together, and for any additional advance preparation information.

Following the visit, meet with your group to discuss what the youth learned and experienced and to answer any questions.

Option 2: Experience a Seder

Many biblical scholars believe that the Last Supper took place during a Seder meal, a special event in the life of Jews when they remember God's deliverance and redemption. Our Communion services still contain elements of the early Seder dinners, but experiencing a Seder dinner brings a new dimension to one's understanding of the sacrament of Communion.

The order of service for a Seder dinner is called *Haggadah*, and hundreds of them have been written. The word *haggadah* means to tell or to relate. The *Haggadah* is a vivid narrative that tells the story of the birth of the Jews as a people. It deals primarily with the events in Egypt which led from slavery to liberation. Passover, with the *Haggadah* as its focus, tells every Jew three things: who you are, where you came from, and what you stand for.

Worship Service: A Jewish Worship Experience

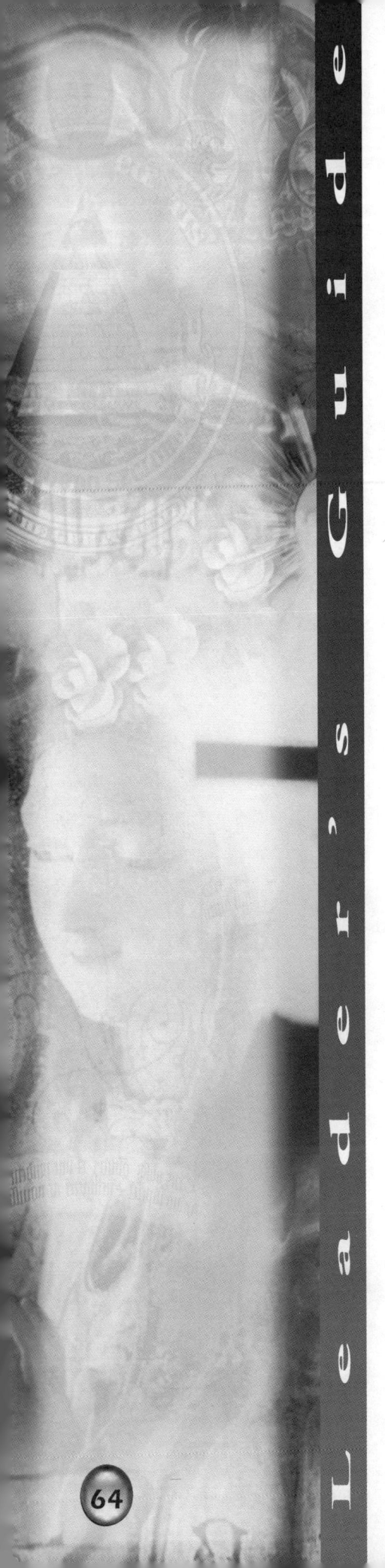

Some *Haggadahs* are very simple and functional, while others are elaborate and require much time and preparation. In addition, a few *Haggadahs* have been specifically written for Christians to remember their Jewish heritage and to consider Jesus' life and ministry in a symbolic way.

Planning and providing a Seder meal for your youth or congregation does require advance preparation such as researching the customs, purchasing the ingredients, preparing some of the elements of the meal, and setting up the table. The Internet is an excellent resource that provides extensive background information, recipes, and orders of worship.

You also may want to prepare a handout for the students. One possibility is to list key words and their meanings. Consider including a summary of the information provided in this article and highlight the connections to our own Christian faith.

It is up to you whether to plan a simple Seder similar to those observed by Jewish families today or to hold a Christian Seder. Check the following websites for help in making your decision.

- **Jewish Seder:** *http://www.holidays.net:80/passover/index.htm*
- **Christian Seder:** *http://www.cresourcei.org/seder.html*

Choosing Jesus: The Real Deal on the Spiritual Menu